The Richest Woman
in the
World

A Trilogy
Book One

by

M.G. Lambert

Published by Principio Books, LLC
14525 SW Millikan Way, #75822
Beaverton, Oregon 97005
info@principiobooks.com
www.principiobooks.com
ISBN: 1629080144
ISBN-13: 978-1-62908-014-7

About the Author

M.G. Lambert grew up and still lives in South Florida, where this trilogy is set, in part.

The author was a public relations and editorial executive for a major U.S. airline for a number of years and was based in Miami, was a writer for Florida and national publications, and has business interests throughout North America. The author has written extensively about American industries founded in the late 1800s and early 1900s.

Other works of fiction by M.G. Lambert include:

The Other Side of Power

Fly with the author into the heart of the airline industry, meet its leaders and their loves, and live through their struggles to survive strikes, business clashes, and terrorism.

On sale now at www.principiobooks.com

Coming soon:

The Richest Woman in the World - Book Two

The Richest Woman in the World - Book Three

Once a Pelican

The Children—a Collection of Short Stories

The War is Over and Other Stories

Franchise

Mae and Percy

and more...

Dedication

This trilogy is dedicated to the author's mother whose riches were her faith, her devotion to her family, and her ability to pray and believe, no matter how great the adversities of her life.

Acknowledgments

The author thanks Meredith E. Bagby, founder and publisher of Principio Books, for her constant encouragement and belief.

The author is extremely grateful to Susan Woitovich for her brilliant production and editing, her ever-constant attention to detail, and her great suggestions for finding just the right word.

Chapter 1

Manhattan, July 17, 1898

Her mother was beaten to death on the floor of a shirt factory on Greene Street—yesterday.

In a charity grave, her mother was laid to rest—today.

Louise Lambert wavered between the reality and the reason of her own existence and the illusion of a shapeless, black horror—tomorrow.

Without anyone else to turn to now, the girl had put her life at the mercy of the two women who were meeting behind the double, grainy oak doors. They might as well have been gods as two mortals with their total, if only temporary, power over her.

It seemed she had been waiting outside the parlor of the brownstone building on West Eighteenth Street for hours. Wringing her hands over and over, she argued with herself—should she nudge one of the doors open to hear? No. If they caught her trying to eavesdrop, they would find a cruel punishment for her. They might even throw her out of the big house to which she had turned for refuge, abandoning her to the infested immigrant squalor south of Fourteenth Street. The hunger, the poverty, the stench below that boundary all waited like fraternity demons ready to seize her for their living march of death.

If you were an immigrant, there was no way of escaping the

seething tenements crammed with factory slaves and pushcart vendors—unless you were a willing young female. Then you did not have to settle for the streets that squatted along the East River. You could sell your bodily wares to men who came downtown to fancy, forbidden houses like Margaret Dugal's.

"Bitch," cried Margaret Dugal, her gravelly voice blasting through the doors. "I put a roof over your head, Cecilia, feed you like a queen, and you try to rob me, rob us all. You ungrateful whore. You're taking bread off my table for this little bastard…"

"I'm just asking you to let her stay here a few nights…give her a damn chance, let her work in the kitchen for her keep, Margaret. She's a child," Cecilia pleaded.

There was no need to crack the doors. Louise's body quivered as she heard every word exchanged between the two women.

"I'm giving her the chance of her life. Tonight she becomes one of my girls, and she'll have more money than she ever dreamed of. Anyway, what's she to you? Ah, yes, an Italian sister. I forgot for a minute. You damned Sicilians stick together like glue."

"She'll be out tomorrow then. I'll find a place for her."

"Will you now? Where? With the Jewish family that threw her out today? Or maybe one of your Italian friends will take her to starve with them. Huh? Or maybe you'll send her back to die in one of those factories where her ma was killed? It's every child and man for himself in the streets today. If you like the girl so much, let her stay here, Cecilia, where at least she'll be able to eat. And damn good, too. Out on the street, she'll be a whore anyway, humping immigrant filth just off the boats…from the ghettos of Europe to the ghettos of New York. Huh? Is that what you want for her?"

"Stop it, Margaret. I'll get her out now."

"Oh, no you won't. You've got no money. I happen to know.

It's not quite payday yet. And you owe me—remember the little loan? Besides, dearie, don't you know what's happened? We've won the war—the word's just out—the Spanish-American War is over. Santiago has surrendered to General Shafter. About now they're playing 'Rally Round the Flag Boys' down there in Cuba, and do you know what that victory means for us?

"Tonight'll be one goddamn traffic jam in this house. And I need every ass I can get. There'll be more money taken in at this house than that girl, what's her name—Louise—will ever see in her lifetime. Speaking about money, Cecilia, I notice you've been spitting on it."

"What are you talking about, Margaret?" Cecilia shouted.

"Ah, don't act so innocent with me. For the past two nights you've turned your little nose up at some of my regulars. Too busy, you say—'Can't handle you tonight.' Well, you little tart..."

It seemed they would never stop arguing over Cecilia's refusal to take on all the men Margaret sent to her room. Louise half-listened, grateful that they had dropped her from their tongue-lashing. Her mind pulled her back away from here. Their voices became echoes. It was yesterday all over again.

If she lived to be 100 years old, Louise would never be able to erase from her mind the smallest detail of her mother's last moments as she lay on the creaking, smutty wood floor of the garment factory.

Nola Lambert's eyes were closed, frozen shut. Her tongue sprang forward, loose, her mouth spewing thick, blue-red blood out over her chin and cheeks and streaming into fissures that stuck to the dark brown strands of her hair, which spread out into an arc around her head.

Gripping her mother, tugging at her, Louise screamed.

"Mama, Mama, don't go. Please, Mama, don't...you can't die, Mama." The girl's sobbing consumed her—Louise's limp, thin figure falling at her mother's side.

With her head resting on Nola's breasts, Louise felt the heat of her mother's flesh and heard what she imagined was the last attempt of her heart to keep pumping. Then, gradually, the rumble, the gurgling of the chains and tunnels of the life forces within her body stopped. Her head fell to one side as if all cords connecting it to her shoulders were slashed. The strong, insistent arms of a fellow female worker clutched the girl, trying to pull her away.

A wave of retreat slid over Louise, making her skin quiver, but she would not let go of her mother. Yet in the same moment she wanted to run from the vile odors of the feces and urine released from the body, seeping from under the long, full skirt and onto the floor. The picture before her was acrid, nauseating. She hated herself for wanting those same strange arms to drag her from the grotesqueness of death. With the next breath, Louise ached for her mother. She seized her, shook her, fell upon her.

Flailing her arms above herself, Louise felt her own body wet from the room bathed in sheets of steam rising from the crush of sweating workers and the gasps of the pressing machines. She shouted, her shrieks filling her head with throbbing bolts of pain.

"Leave us alone. She's dead. My mother's dead," she wailed.

Her only real link with humanity was taken from her. Murdered. She stared around the room crowded with women and dotted here and there with men bared to their waists to withstand the scorching air. They were all blurred through her tears. The room spun, and when she felt herself being moved away from her mother, she relented, almost relieved that someone else was in command of her body.

"God is with her," a woman whispered to her.

"Cry it all out," said another, who squeezed her hand until it stung.

For the first time in her 14 years, Louise had lost control of herself, and she could not muster the power to walk.

There was a great frenzy all about her, with the cries of the women making her pain more—and then less. Abruptly, the chorus of mourners was broken by a guttural tongue.

"I did not do it. I did not kill her. She was sick and she fell. She would not finish the work so I hit…only once. I did not know she was sick. It was an accident." The man seemed to Louise to be pleading with the sea of terrified eyes surrounding him. "It was a goddamn accident," he kept shouting, socking his dark, hair-covered hand into the air.

No one answered him. He was the boss. This could have happened to other workers or to Louise, who came daily to this place after school to gather remnants of fabric for the factory to be sold in pushcarts on Orchard Street.

Mr. Kalish had struck workers before. Her mother told her of the beatings in the factory, of the women who fainted from the heat, of the pressers who coughed from tuberculosis. She had never told the girl of any death. But now…

Over the last few months, her mother had grown pale. Broken blue veins etched spider-like webs on her legs and hands. She was exhausted most of the time Louise spent with her.

Nola was still a beautiful woman, and this was not Louise's opinion alone, she knew. Men came to their small flat to call and to take Nola out on Saturday nights and Sunday afternoons. Nola left the girl with neighbors some nights. Louise could remember when her mother did not come back for her at all but picked her up in the mornings.

"Well," her mother would say, "I have to have a little companionship. One day I may even get married and you may have a daddy." But she never married or had a serious man. Children, neighbors said, drove men away from even pretty women.

"I have a decent job, Louise, to support us," Nola told her when another suitor faded away. "I like this job, and no one cares if I am fat here. They are all mothers, big and heavy, and they are all from the old countries—Poland, Russia, Ireland, Italy. We sew and we laugh together." There was no smile on her face, though, as she traced her days for Louise at supper.

Louise pictured her mother as she prepared for work each morning before five. After brushing her long, shiny brown hair, she would twist it and then twirl it into a donut shape at the back of her head. Wisps of lighter hair, almost blonde, framed her wide, smooth face. Her green eyes, flecked with bits of brown, danced when she told Louise about her home in Sicily. That was usually at night by candlelight as she feathered Louise's cheeks with her long, slender fingers, fingers that never stopped their chores—sewing, cleaning, cooking, soothing.

"Stop pedaling the machines, Mama," the girl remembered begging her, "and stop sewing."

"How can I stop, my child? We have to eat. To sew sleeves into shirts at the factory is my job. It is what I have learned. I am lucky to have work, with people starving in the streets all around. It is all I can do, Louise. We will be all right."

Like the other shopmasters on Greene Street, Mr. Kalish was a thrashing monster, grinding humans in his path. These people, Louise and her mother, were at his mercy. When her mother could not go on working at the speed he demanded, he beat her. The workers told Louise about the final incident which had occurred just minutes before she arrived from school. He struck the last blow to her mother's suffering, to her misery here in this dungeon. He was a murderer. Would he go on killing? Who would stop Mr. Kalish, the beast who controlled these men and women who had to make their wages here just to survive?

Louise was too weak to think about his punishment. The police would do that. Wasn't there justice for everyone? Every day in school, Mrs. Cavalani told her students there was equality for all in America. And Louise believed the promise. So did her mother.

When the police came, the workers started to move away from the body, watching as the two tall men—dark-suited, apple-cheeked, Irish—cut their ways through the crowd and knelt by Nola.

The police did not seem to listen to Mr. Kalish who shouted on, his face and bare, hairy chest sopping with sweat. The pair of policemen looked at each other, and one of them motioned to the doorway of the dark room lighted only by a few naked, low-hung electric bulbs. A narrow stretcher topped with gray, folded blankets and white sheets seemed to slip from nowhere through the people.

"Mama," the girl shouted. Her head flew back as she sank against the fat women who held her hands and arms.

When Louise awoke, she stared into a wide, olive-skinned face punctuated with small, dark brown eyes and a smiling mouth crowded with white teeth. A puffy, short-fingered hand pushed Louise's hair from around her face and gently rubbed the skin of her forehead with a cold, damp cloth.

"Mrs. Robolenko," Louise said, a question in her voice.

"Yes, yes, you are safe," the woman nodded. "Here. Eat." From a small green crockery bowl, chipped around the rim, she took a spoon and held it to the girl's mouth. Louise brought her body forward, held the soup bowl, and bit into the piece of dark bread Mrs. Robolenko gave her.

"Papa brought you from the factory. You stay the night here," she said.

Looking around the small room of the Robolenko flat she had come to know from playing with the six children who lived here, Louise thought of her own flat a building away. Jumping up, she knew she must get home. "I have to get home." She held her hands to her head, remembering…

"No, no. Time to stay here and eat supper with us," Mrs. Robolenko said. Taking the girl by the hand, she led her to a sofa where they sat for a few minutes until Louise could no longer stand the lumps and the broken springs pushing against her body.

"Go out on the escape for air," the woman told her, rubbing her eyes with the bottom corner of her apron. "It's going to be better tomorrow. The pain will pass."

Louise could not talk to even this kind woman. Not now.

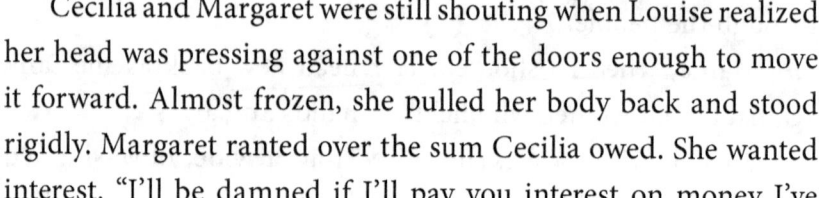

Cecilia and Margaret were still shouting when Louise realized her head was pressing against one of the doors enough to move it forward. Almost frozen, she pulled her body back and stood rigidly. Margaret ranted over the sum Cecilia owed. She wanted interest. "I'll be damned if I'll pay you interest on money I've owed for a week," Cecilia yelled.

Now, Louise wanted them to get back to her. Where would she go? Why didn't she just run away from New York? Where to? Where to? Her thoughts drifted again.

It seemed months ago—and it was only hours—that she

stood on the fire escape of the Robolenko place near her own apartment on Cherry Street. Alone on the iron rack, she waited for Berel and Esther Robolenko to dress their six children and get them off to school. In the flat, she was only in the way as she had been the night before lying with Sarah, the 12-year-old, on her cot. Louise had not slept at all or eaten a bite of the rolled cabbage and potatoes Mrs. Robolenko put in front of her as supper at the round table in the kitchen.

The sounds of Yiddish fading into English and back again into the strange language disturbed Louise as she lay, one leg and one arm hanging off the side of the thin mattress, to make room for Sarah's plump body.

"She can't stay here. We have so many mouths to feed now, Esther. Even with our Hannah dead, and God rest this girl's mother, we can't do it, we can't keep this extra child," Mr. Robolenko kept saying.

He was not lying. How Mr. Robolenko provided for his big family on his wages at the factory where her mother worked baffled Nola, Louise recalled. Yet Louise would give anything to stay in this small box with its smelly children who bathed only once a week—if then—with its greasy, big iron stove, its metal beds in tiers, with soiled down comforters, and patched pillows. And above all, with its mama, fat and warm, and its papa, gray-bearded, round, hardworking. But she knew she could not live with them.

As Louise leaned on the railing of the fire escape watching fresh-hung laundry flap on lines suspended from other Jewish flats at the rear of the five-story tenement, she thought of the wash at her own building. Reds, yellows, greens, blues. Bright, happy colors—Italian. You could always tell a building's nationality by its laundry. Yiddish was dull—gray, black, dark blue.

She was often proud to be Italian. She did not belong in a Jewish building anyway. In the back of her mind was the realization that she had to find Cecilia as her mother always told her to do if anything should happen to Nola.

After the funeral, attended only by a few factory workers, Mrs. Robolenko kissed the girl's cheeks; her husband shook her hand. There were no tears from them. The Robolenkos knew death well. Three months ago, their daughter, Hannah, was struck and killed by an ice truck rounding a corner where she stood. Mr. Robolenko's father and mother burned to death in their apartment on Montgomery Street the first of the year.

There was talk that Berel and Esther would help her if she could not find Cecilia, but Louise knew they were burdened by their own lives, and she could not ask them for anything more. She was lucky to have been befriended by them at all.

At her flat, separated from the Robolenkos by buildings housing Poles and Russians, she packed a canvas bag with her two dresses, some underwear, stockings, and an old straw hat with blue ribbons—her mother's. Louise needed to find something else of her mother's—yes, the white handkerchief she always carried in her pocket. She found the small square of linen on a closet shelf and falling from the folds was a small silver cross and chain that Nola rarely wore. Louise squeezed the cross in her fist. This was her saving grace. In her tragedy she had almost forgotten the only piece of jewelry Nola owned.

Louise turned over the key to the flat to the manager of the building, who would, he said, have to keep everything to pay for the rent due.

Louise's eyes filled with tears as she looked around the single room that had been her home, the only one she had ever known. Two chairs whose green threads were worn through to the cotton stuffing, some dented metal pots, a black iron skillet, a wooden rack of dresses, most of them old and too small for her mother in recent years. "Everything stays here," the man kept saying, fidgeting with his ring of keys. When he closed and locked the door behind them and the girl followed him down the dark, narrow hall, Louise felt an emptiness that she knew she would never be able to forget.

She did not know how she had gotten uptown to this house on Eighteenth Street, but somehow her body had managed to make the movements for her. She touched her arms, sore from carrying her bag. Reaching in her pocket, she rubbed Nola's cross.

Her mother described this house as a furnace of sex. And yet it was the place where Louise's body was created. That made the house special, didn't it? Or was it really a kind of hell? Was she damned by her conception in this brothel?

"Don't think about that. It's only a building. I might have been anywhere to have you planted in me," her mother said when Louise brought up the question.

Would her mother be here now, still a prostitute, if she had not made her "mistake" at Margaret Dugal's?

"When you get pregnant, you are finished in this business. At least at Margaret Dugal's. I can't blame her. Look at me." These words and her gesture of patting her wide, well-padded hips and tapping her full bosom were one of her mother's rituals. She seemed not to be speaking to her daughter but reminding herself that she was not marketable flesh at Margaret's any more. Nola still went to Margaret's—to visit Cecilia, who always welcomed Nola and Louise at a side door. Louise's eyes were always drawn to the wide, red-carpeted stairway which led to darkness at the top—a kind of sanctuary of mystery and of her birth.

Cecilia and Nola would sit laughing and talking in a small room off the entrance hall while Louise played on the polished wood floor at their feet with Margaret's old bull dog, O'Reilly. Margaret was usually out when Nola and Louise paid visits, and only twice did Louise catch a glimpse of Margaret, whose face looked just like her dog's.

Cecilia and Nola had come to America together. For a quick, unguarded second, Louise hated them both for believing the promises of the New York political bosses who arranged for thousands of Italian girls like her mother to sail in the holds of cattle boats to America. Unskilled, young, ignorant, and foreign-tongued, they were only too agreeable to settle in the houses these men controlled. Had these young innocents any idea of how they were to be used, Louise wondered.

Was this the American dream the old, bent, craggy-skinned Italians in Lower Manhattan described in their broken, confused English? Was this the American glory Mrs. Cavalani pounded into Louise's head every day?

Sometimes, Louise was relieved she was not 100 percent Italian—most of them whom she knew were pathetically gullible. Except for Cecilia, who seemed apart from the poverty engulfing everyone around her. Even Louise's mother.

As Louise stood with one hand flat against the door of the parlor, she vowed she would escape these trenches filled with stupid Italians and Irishmen and Jews...and whore houses like Margaret's...someday. She would not only get even for her mother's killing, she would rise so high that those who hurt her would glorify the very slums that spawned her.

A deep, severe anger swelled within Louise and drove her to another dawn.

Chapter 2

Cecilia finally gave in. Yes, she would pay the interest Margaret demanded and more—if only she would let Louise stay tonight. Tomorrow was another day, and somehow she would find a place for the girl, she promised. Margaret's voice showed signs of relenting or was Louise misreading her: Why didn't they get on with this and call her in and tell her what was to happen?

If Cecilia had no money, would she have to borrow more? Surely she had some coins. Even Louise had a quarter and some pennies in her pocket. They would not get her a room, but they would buy her a bite to eat, at least for tonight.

How long had she been standing out here, ten minutes, half an hour? What did time matter though? She had no destination at all.

Maybe she could stay here as a kitchen girl or maid. Her thoughts glossed over being a prostitute. After all, what did she know of men? And what she had seen repulsed her.

In her tenement with only one toilet every other floor, it was impossible for her to avoid seeing men's private parts now and then. It was common to see men pulling out their penises to urinate on fire escapes or along the staircase of her building if they did not have windows in their flats. Louise always tried not to notice such behavior—it usually made her sick to her stomach.

There were encounters she had not been able to avoid. She winced when a picture of Mr. Punnello flashed before her.

Already late for school one morning, she swung a bathroom door open to find him dangling his long, red penis over the toilet, and then, grinning at her, he held it up in both hands and howled. Stunned by this man who had been kind to her on the front steps of the house, giving her fruits and candies often, she fled, screaming down the hall, all the way back to her flat.

Mr. Punnello tormented her after that, exposing himself to her every chance he could. Louise was actually glad when he fell down the shaft of a pulley lift and died at a factory where he worked as a cloak maker. It was just punishment, Louise consoled herself. Second thoughts made her ashamed for her evil wanderings.

In third grade, two years later, a Polish boy cornered Louise in a school supply room, forcing her to pull down her leg-long bloomers while he ripped open his pants and pulled out his soft, stinking organ. Kicking at his penis with her shoe, Louise knocked the boy over, and his head hit the wall, stunning him. He never bothered her again. Why were boys and men always trying to show themselves to her? It hurt to remember such experiences, and yet she could not help herself; she could not shut out these ugly sights.

In a way, Louise was glad she had not known her father. He was probably like all the rest of the males she had encountered.

"Your pa was a handsome French sailor and I loved him, Louise. I did love your papa. He went away, and I never saw him to tell him about you, but you have his name and I took it, too. It's a good, pretty name, Lambert," her mother's words came ringing back to the girl. Tears welled in her eyes when she remembered her mother's story of how she came to be. Louise had never told anyone she was a bastard. How could she bring herself to admit she was nothing more than an accident, some remnant of bought, wild passion? That she did not know her father and probably never would? Anyway, how could Nola be sure the Frenchman was her father when she slept with scores of men?

All the girl knew was that Nola Lambert was a good mother. She fed her child well and clothed her and sent her to school and kept her from life on the streets where many of Louise's friends had learned to steal their food and clothes and to sell their bodies to anyone with a few nickels and dimes.

The girl's head swam with confusion. Maybe she would be better off out there in the streets. I was wrong to come here, Louise told herself. She had no right to burden Cecelia, to force her to confront Margaret Dugal. Cecilia should never have told Margaret what happened to Louise, whose story made the girl open prey to the old witch.

Louise blinked as she looked at the bronze, overhead light fixture. Electric lights—Louise and her mother had never been able to afford them in their flat. They were fortunate at Margaret Dugal's to have such a luxury.

There was a long silence as she braced her body against the table to the left of the doors. Glancing down at the shiny wood floor, she studied the feet of the table, lion claws. Louise shuddered. She felt as if she were going to be mangled any second, and those intricately carved paws would drip with her blood. Did people who were about to be executed feel this way? It was not so much the gallows as the expectation of death, she thought. If they would just get it over, tell her what was to become of her.

If only she had a friend, someone who could take her in for a night or two, then she might be able to find a way to cope with her life. More than anything she wanted to run home to the closet-sized tenement room she had shared with her mother, to hide from Mrs. Dugal, and to free Cecilia from trying to save her...

"One night, then, that's all she has free, and then she goes to work just like the rest of us. That's final. And if you mess with me any more, I will see that tonight she is put to work," Margaret Dugal shouted, "and not in any kitchen, mind you, but in bed, where she belongs."

There was a pause, and then the woman started yelling at Cecilia again. "I will never understand you, Cecilia, trying to save the daughter of a slut. Look how she died. You can't tell me it was one of them factory beatings. The boss probably got tired of her, and at that she was probably giving it to him for free, stupid ass...you can't save people, Cecilia. Don't you know that? Remember, she came here to me of her own free will. I didn't go out and drag her into my house by the hair of her little head."

"I'll take your damn abuse for now, Margaret, because I have to, but there will come a day when I will see you beg me. Remember that, you old bat," Cecilia yelled. "The girl did not come here because she wanted to be a prostitute. She had nowhere else in this damn world to go."

So Cecilia had won. Louise did have a place for the night. She was safe for another day.

Yet what was Cecilia planning? Where would she send Louise after tonight? Maybe she and Cecilia could run away together. She would repay Cecilia for standing by her when no one else on earth cared about her. Oh, it was ridiculous now to think of helping anyone else, wasn't it. She was a lone, helpless girl of 14 with no skills, no relatives, no decent way of making a way for herself.

Louise shook her head. She must be crazy to envision that she would ever be in a position to have any say over another person's life or for that matter to chart even her own destiny. You are out of your head to imagine the things you do, she told herself. Her stomach was beginning to make gnawing sounds, and she remembered she had not eaten since yesterday afternoon. She was weak. Her head vibrated with pain, and she felt every other minute that she would faint.

Letting go of the knob with her hand almost frozen into a clutching position, she stepped back from the doors and stood with her spine against the lion-clawed table, waiting for Cecelia and Margaret to emerge. She knew at least what awaited her tonight, but she was not strong enough to worry beyond that.

Cecilia made her exit from the parlor first, kicking one of the doors so hard the sound made Louise jump. Her dark eyes flashed when she caught sight of Louise, her voice fell, and she reached for Louise's hand. "Come with me into the kitchen, Louise," she said.

With her head lowered, Louise followed the young woman who seemed to be in command now. With a jerk of her head, Louise peered back at the fat Margaret Dugal who stood like a boulder between the open doors of the parlor. Wobbling toward Cecilia and Louise, Margaret screamed so that her cries echoed in the space between herself and the hallway where the younger women stopped in their tracks.

"This is my house, Cecilia, and I will give the orders here. Not you. Come back here, the both of you, and look me in the eye," Margaret yelled, glaring at them.

Margaret Dugal was a tall, round woman with a mop of maroon hair piled atop her heavily jowled face. Margaret did not blink, her eyes staring blankly ahead as if they were not focusing. She was thick-lipped and exaggerated this feature even more by smearing on a rose-colored lip rouge which spread into the fine cracks of her skin just under her nose and above her chin. Except for the smudges of color on her cheeks and lips, Margaret looked to Louise as if someone had dunked her face into a barrel of flour.

Looking down at her ankle-high, brown, laced shoes and the hem of her blue skirt which skimmed the tops of her shoes, Louise did not want to meet Margaret's eyes. She knew she must—that was an order.

Louise glanced up as Margaret was taking a white handkerchief from the bulging bosom of her shiny, red, low-cut gown. Shaking the white cloth out in front of her, Margaret smiled, revealing yellow-brown teeth set far apart and blotched with her lip rouge. When Margaret reached out to feel Louise's long hair, the girl pulled back from the pointed red fingernails she saw coming toward her.

"Don't be afraid, my dearie. I am just admiring your black locks, the blackest hair I've ever seen," she said, rubbing together a handful of Louise's curls. "Your eyes are the bluest to cross my path in many years. Such looks may carry you far—if you ever get started, Louise." Then the old woman cackled and cocked her head back, obviously amused at her prediction, Louise thought.

Louise looked at Cecilia, hoping she would tear them away from Margaret's glazed stare. Even in the intense July heat, Cecilia was perfectly composed, Louise noticed. She stood straight and motionless in her long purple dress which fell gracefully to the floor from her small waist. She seemed more a picture than a live person standing there, her head tilted, her arms folded loosely in front of her.

"Leave me alone, Margaret," Cecilia said. "I am your best girl, your drawing card, and you know it. I could take this house away from you, and you know that, too."

"Ha," Margaret shouted, waving her arms about. The stale, flowery scent of Margaret's talc filled the air, and Louise felt nauseous from it but managed to hold back the vomit she tasted. "You wouldn't with this little number in my stable, now would you? Is that what all the fuss is really about, Cecilia?"

Margaret waited, putting her hands on her hips. "Your threats are as empty as your head, you know that? Where would you get money enough to take this house away from the great Margaret Dugal of Eighteenth Street, huh? From one of your fancy men? Thugs like Paul Kelly's cronies or maybe Monk Eastman's? Maybe you ought to check in again at New Brighton's, and you could take this little Italian sausage with you. I can do without you and her and the lot of you to be born. I own this place and every stick of furniture in it. Nobody controls me. I don't pay nobody off any more."

"I know your connections through Tammany Hall, Mrs. Dugal, and don't forget I know some of them better than you do," Cecilia said with a calmness and power in her voice that made Louise feel more secure.

"Violet," shouted Margaret, her hot, rotten breath shooting into Louise's face. "Come here and bring my salts."

"Don't tell me you feel a spell coming on, Margaret?" Cecilia said.

"Violet!" Margaret yelled again.

A tall, boney Negro woman with graying hair pulled back straight and bound in a tight knot at the back of her head, ran to Margaret's side. In her hand was a small, padded square of cheesecloth. The Negress held it up to Margaret's nose. Gripping the black woman's arm, Margaret breathed heavily of the salts.

"Violet, get me to a chair. Now! Now!" Margaret stuck her

handkerchief back into the front of her dress as Violet put her long arms around Margaret's shoulders and helped her back to the parlor. Cecilia and Louise followed them into the front room where the lingering odors of cigar smoke and whisky closed in on Louise. The staleness had accumulated over many years, Louise imagined, as she tried to keep from breathing in the dank, putrid air.

"I'm, I'm going to faint, Violet. Quick, quick…I, I…" Margaret gasped and fell to her knees and then crumpled into a heap on the floor. Violet caught her head and held it, applying the square of salts to her nose.

Margaret reminded Louise of a washed-ashore whale, lying there, her blubbery body motionless. Was she dead? Louise looked at Cecilia who was bending to feel Margaret's pulse at the wrist and to lift her eyelids.

"She's all right," Cecilia said. "The heat and anger. Blood pressure problem. She always has it in the summer. No need to call the doctor. Keep the salts to her nose, and we'll give her a whisky later."

Violet nodded. "I know you are right, Miss Cecilia. Reckon we ought to move her to the settee?"

"Yes, lift her from underneath. Louise, lend a hand."

Louise knelt down and with Cecilia and Violet raised the dead weight of the woman off the floor and up to the long piece of amber, satin-covered furniture. The settee was wide, and when Margaret's body was heaved upon it, the cushions sank deeper into its frame. One of Margaret's arms dangled to the side, falling toward the floor.

Motioning with a finger, Cecilia backed up to the door of the parlor, turned and led Violet and Louise outside to the vestibule.

Cecilia took folded bills from a small, white-beaded purse, fringed at the bottom with long gold threads, and handed the money to Violet.

"I want you to put the girl in the small room on the third floor, Violet." Cecilia winked at the dark woman who nodded at the instructions. "I don't want you to hurry Miss Margaret's recovery, Violet. I'll say again there's no need to call the doctor. Don't let Miss Margaret near this child. You understand? I'll stop at nothing to get your neck if you do, Vi." Then in the next breath, "But, if you follow my orders, there'll be more money for you. You know I'm good about paying, don't you , Vi?" Cecilia patted her purse, and the Negress smiled and nodded her head in agreement.

So Cecilia did have money after all, or did Margaret just provide more?

Louise watched as Cecilia moved to the front door. To Louise, Cecilia was a Charles Dana Gibson magazine cover come to life, with her soft features and folds of up-swept hair.

Cecilia stood for a moment silhouetted against the frosted glass of the door, looking intently at Louise.

"I don't want to stay here without you, Cecilia," Louise pleaded.

"You'll have to, Louise. I have an important errand. I promise I will come back soon." She motioned the girl to her and put her hands on Louise's shoulders. "Stay in the room Violet takes you to. She will bring you some food. If Margaret tries to hurt you, tie you up, run." Her voice was hushed and low so that Violet could not hear, Louise knew. "Run as fast as you can to the little church on Sixteenth Street at the corner. Stay there and wait for help. Do you understand?"

"Yes, Cecilia, yes," Louise managed to answer, a thickness in her throat. As Cecilia left the house, Louise felt lost all over again.

Sitting in the box of a room on the third floor of Margaret Dugal's, the girl could not stop the aching fear that raced to the pit of her stomach. Would Violet keep Margaret from her as she was paid to do? After all, Margaret was the owner of the house, and Violet's first allegiance was to her, not to Cecilia. Louise's chest tightened as she pictured Margaret's coming after her. No, she told herself, Violet will not let Margaret come in.

Her thoughts raced ahead—if Cecilia did not come back here, what would she do? Run to the church? For what? Who there would help her? Her mother took her to mass on Christmas Eve and on Easter; still she felt awkward in church, guilty for not taking communion, for not confessing her sins. Maybe one day she would build the courage to walk into any church any time.

If no one at the church could offer aid, then what? She could be a cook like Violet or a maid, couldn't she?

Quickly, Louise's hopes fell. The country was still recovering from the depression of 1893. Company failures in the thousands, bank closings, the financial crash of the railroads, strikes by steel-workers and miners all filtered through the classes that made up America. Jobs were so scarce that anyone lucky enough to work did not complain about long hours or poor wages or anything. Adults got first chances at jobs, so why would Louise even be considered by any employer? No one would hire a girl so young and inexperienced. Her work at Mr. Kalish's had not been a real job. Pipe dreams—every thought of employment was imaginary. She should shut out all foolish thoughts and concentrate on the grim realities of her life.

Louise felt of the thin mattress on which she sat and the dulled brass of the bedstead. Wonder how many people have slept here? The thought of the multitudes of men and women who had made love on this bed made her sink into an abyss of depression.

Perhaps, she thought, my own mother…no, I must stop this. She shook her head.

Lucia Caruso—I wonder what she's doing now. Yes, my best friend is packing lace, boxes and boxes of delicate lace that Venetians had made for centuries. Her fingers are raw from handling it, but she is able to make a few pennies to take home to her parents and she is very proud. The nine children, including Lucia, are too hungry to know gratefulness or to thank Lucia, the eldest sibling. There are so many of them, maggots when they are all at home, climbing over one another, sleeping in human piles. Their dreary flat on Mulberry Bend was so far away in time from Louise that the sounds of their laughter and their constant noise were just visions now.

Despite their lack of everything, the Caruso family, like the Robolenkos, was always together, and somehow there was always enough bread to go around their big table. While she could not ask them to take her in, she could ask Lucia to help her find work at one of the other factories. No, she caught herself before she fabricated any longer. My mother died in one of those places, and I will not go near any of them. I will never walk on Greene Street again.

Most of her past was so dark that she must learn to control her memories. A brighter glimpse came to her. She thought of her mother at her bedside, reliving her own childhood in Sicily. As her mother's soft voice described the sunny days there and the fishing boats returning to port laden with heavy catches, Louise would fall asleep, hoping she would go to Sicily one day and live out her life there. No more freezing winters in New York in rooms without heat. No more gray days for Louise. She would live on fish and fruit and wine made by the villagers, and she would dance forever in the full splendor of the never-ending sun.

The sun, where was it now? Was it afternoon yet? Louise paced around the bed, her body wringing wet from the heat and the closeness of the windowless room. Besides the bed, there was only a small white table and a clear glass lamp topped with a yellowed white shade. When Louise heard voices at the door, she stood back against the near wall so that if the door were opened she would be behind it.

"I don't care how sick she is, Violet, I'll have a look for myself. Out of my way now," Margaret Dugal said.

Louise cringed. How could she be on her feet and up those flights of stairs so soon after her spell? What did Margaret mean by that word, 'sick'? Maybe they had the wrong room.

"She is sick in the monthly way, Miss Margaret. I don't think you want to see that," Violet said.

"Is this some scheme of Cecilia's? If it is, you'll both pay for your lies to me."

"It's the truth, Miss Margaret."

"Open the door this minute, Violet."

In the next second, the door was flung open, and the knob hit Louise in the stomach as it bolted against her.

"So you're sick, huh?"

Violet stared wild-eyed at the girl.

"Yes, yes, I am, Miss Margaret."

"Well, that don't matter to some of my customers. They never see anything in the dark anyways..."

"I'm sorry you were sick, Miss Margaret," Louise said.

"I don't fall for that stuff. Besides, I wasn't so sick, but that's none of your affair. So, you're nice and cozy waiting for your friend, Cecilia. Well, we'll see who wins this battle, won't we now?" Margaret laughed, her belly shaking, her hideous teeth fully exposed.

Violet stood to the side and behind Margaret, and Louise watched the Negress's face for some sign of instruction, but she was obviously frozen with fear. Violet bit her lips, looking at Louise.

"Lie down on the bed, Louise," Margaret ordered the girl. "I don't believe you're sick in the monthly way…"

"Please, Miss Margaret, you don't want to look at…" Violet said.

"It's all right, Violet," the girl said, trying to hide her terror. Gripping the mattress with both hands, Louise stiffened as she lay back on the bed and stared up at Margaret Dugal. Her nightmares were coming true, weren't they? It would be so easy now, Louise thought, to kick the old woman in the face with the heels of her shoes. And then she could run to the church as Cecilia had instructed her. Could she escape, though, down the stairs? Violet might not run after her, but what about someone else in the house? Margaret had men around, bodyguards. She had heard about them from her mother. No, she would not move… not yet…

Margaret Dugal folded her arms, turning from the bed. "Do you two think I want to see a bloody ass? Get up, girl. Give her a bath, Violet. She reeks. I don't want to be any closer than what I've been," Margaret said, seeming to brush aside the confrontation with a stroke of her hand. "When you finish with her, put her right back in here and lock the door. Don't try anything, Louise, or I promise I'll stop you."

When Margaret's last steps faded on the stairway, Louise rose and followed Violet to a room down the hall. Standing before the porcelain tub with curved legs, Violet shook her head at the girl. "You better do what Miss Margaret says now and…wait for Miss

Cecilia. If you run, Miss Louise, I wouldn't want to think about what might happen to you."

Louise nodded. Violet was right, yet she couldn't stay here for long. "What time is it, Violet?" the girl asked as she finished bathing herself.

"Supper time, just about. I know you're hungry, but I got orders from Miss Margaret…"

"I just wonder where Cecilia would be at this time of day."

"I just don't know. I thought she'd be back by now. I guess you're going to have to stay here for the time being."

That inner voice that had spoken to her so often before came to Louise again. She could not remain here no matter what might happen to her as she tried to escape.

"I have to leave you alone now, Miss Louise. Don't try to break away."

Louise could not reveal her plan to Violet. After all, Violet had already had to betray Cecilia, and whether her actions came from stupidity or fear, she would have to account for them. Hadn't Cecilia paid her and warned her clearly?

After Violet left her in the small room, Louise sat on the edge of the bed. She was afloat in a sea of thorns, wasn't she? Rising, she felt the walls for any weakness or secret, movable part. Beating her fist against the white plaster, she began to cry, but as soon as her tears started to flow, Louise realized that allowing herself the weakness of breaking down would destroy her. She must think with her head, not her heart, her mother always reminded her. Poor Mama never seemed able to live by her own advice.

Louise heard a key at her door, was it Violet, she prayed.

There was a whisper. "It's me, Cecilia, Louise."

"Cecilia," the girl cried, and threw her arms around the young woman whose body was hot; her dress drenched with sweat.

"Be quiet and listen, Louise. I have a few minutes, and then I have to get down to the supper table or Margaret will give me the roughest customers of the night. If Margaret comes up here, do anything to her until you can get past her and then run. If she does not come up here—and I pray she doesn't—stay here until I rap on the door three times. That will be before dawn, and then you will be able to find your way to the house of Mr. Henry Flagler on Fifth Avenue and Fifty-Fourth Street. Here's some money. Maybe you can get a ride up there on a milk wagon. No need to be afraid of the men who drive the wagons."

Sitting on her knees on the bed, Louise could not believe Cecilia had found a place for her already. "What am I to do there, Cecilia, at the house on Fifth Avenue? Who is Henry Flagler?"

"A very rich man, Louise, a partner of John Rockefeller. You've heard of him. I know you have. In school you've studied…"

"Yes, and Mr. Flagler is his partner."

"In oil. I have to hurry now. The reason I want you to stay the night is for your own protection, unless you see old Dugal. Then you'll have to get out and, well, just hide where you can until sunup. Wandering around the filthy streets here is no good especially tonight. Let's hope you won't have to. Now, when you get to the Flagler place—it's a huge gray stone mansion—go around back, not to the front door, and ask for Mrs. O'Donnell. She's in charge of the kitchen, and you'll be a worker there. It's a fine chance, Louise. You'll live in a grand house and have good food."

"Cecilia," the girl hugged her friend again. "I owe you my life, Cecilia. I won't forget…"

"No, no, you haven't left here safe yet. If you stayed here, Louise, you would soon grow used to this life, and you'd never be able to leave it. You get in a rut, you see. You can't leave somehow. It's the money. Look at me. No matter what, don't come here again. Never, never look back once you leave a place like this. You're going into…into a better world. I wish I could go with you, but it's too late for me."

"You could get out, Cecilia!"

"No," Cecilia said, touching the girl's long black hair. "Do what they tell you. Work hard. Be clean. Obey Mrs. O'Donnell. She's the best kind of woman I'm told by somebody who knows her well. Mrs. O'Donnell knows all about your mother, where you come from."

"I will do everything they tell me at the Flagler house, Cecilia."

"I know Violet didn't feed you. I know what happened. Violet told me."

"Will you punish Violet?"

"No, she'll just be in my debt for another favor or two. That's the way I have to work with her, keep her owing. Maybe someday I'll have my own maid. One day when I own a house like this myself. Who knows?"

"I could work for you then, couldn't I?"

"No, Louise, you could not. Go to the Flagler house and make a new life. Being a maid, a good maid, can be a fine job. I have to go and don't try to tell me good-bye later. One more thing—you'll hear strange noises and loud people tonight. Don't be frightened by anything, except the old bitch. All right? Good luck, Louise. God knows you deserve some good fortune in your little life." Cecilia knelt down to kiss the girl's forehead.

"I love you, Cecilia. I will always love you."

Turning away abruptly, Cecilia wiped at her eyes with a hand-kerchief, and then she was gone from the room, and Louise did not hear her footsteps on the stairs. They were too soft, Louise thought.

Louise longed to cling to Cecilia, to sob in her arms, to tell her how much she appreciated the new start Cecilia had spun out of air. For a few minutes after Cecilia left her, Louise looked in the direction of the electric light. The heat from the small bulb intensified the close, musty air of the room. She wondered how Cecilia had made such preparations so quickly; then she remembered her mother told her Cecilia had many friends in high places in the city. Why did she stay here and take Margaret's abuse? Why didn't she marry one of the men who came here and paid for her love?

There were so many things Louise did not understand about life, but now was no time to try to solve them. She must remain on the alert every second and be ready to spring into action with the slightest sound of intrusion.

Yes, I must follow Cecilia's instructions exactly.

As she sat on the bed, her knees tucked under her, Louise tried to remember the course of events which had led her here. Yesterday seemed a million years ago. Louise's head spun; she was dizzy from hunger. The future—what about that? There would be no more school for her. What would Mrs. Cavalani do with her pencil box, her books, her slate when the school ended for the summer next week? She pictured the teacher's frowning face as she asked the class, "Do you know where Louise Lambert is today? Her mother died, so maybe she has moved away. Her things—I will keep them for now. She will come back."

The girl who sat in row five, seat four at P.S. 40 did not exist any longer, Louise thought. Soon, everyone in class would try to solve the mystery of her disappearance, and no one would ever be able to find any trace of her. It would be as if she never, ever existed. Well, she told herself, someday she would make them all aware that she was alive and that no one could destroy her—not Margaret Dugal, not this house or the men in it, not the factory boss that killed her mother. No one.

Chapter 3

Margaret Dugal's big house rumbled, vibrated, and shook as if it were being hurled about by some furious beast. Her eyes fixed on the door of the little room where she waited for Cecilia's knock, Louise was sure that any minute the plaster of the walls would come crashing down around her. Never, not even on Saturday nights in her tenement, had she heard such screaming, laughter, raucousness. The people she knew cried out from sickness, hunger, anger—but not from this kind of sensual wildness.

In their alcoholic stupors, the men in Margaret Dugal's house were yelling from the pursuit and quick satisfaction of physical pleasure mostly unknown, she thought, to the poor of the ghettos. At least she had not heard such howling.

How strange, she thought, to be driven to the point that you leave the privacy of your own soul and body and reveal your inner longings and gratification to everyone around you. Such release was different when you were crammed in tenement boxes, for somehow letting your frustrations and energies burst forth brought a wave of quiet relief—that is what Louise's mother had told her.

The people on the floors below her must be falling down

drunk—which should make her getaway much simpler. Then there was Margaret Dugal, who seemed to smell all plans contrary to her own. Margaret had not come to her door yet. That was a blessing.

Louise prayed that Mrs. O'Donnell was nothing like Margaret. Yet if she happened to be, then what? What if the rich people she was going to work for gave parties that produced the kind of behavior common at Margaret Dugal's? Did Mr. Flagler entertain permissive men and women? Was he dedicated to reckless living? Drinking? She wished Cecilia had told her more about him and his household. But then what choice did Louise have anyway and what right had she to question those who were so powerful and rich?

John D. Rockefeller was one of the most important men in the country—she had read about him and the Standard Oil Company at school, but she could not remember Mr. Flagler's name from her books. If he was a partner of Mr. Rockefeller, though, he had to be a giant in the business world. How would she speak to such a man and his family? Was he old or young, handsome, ugly? He was probably very good looking, and his family must all be brilliant and beautiful, bejeweled, and exquisitely dressed.

Rich—the word made her mind churn with questions. How much money did you have to have to be rich? She could not guess what measuring stick one used in proclaiming richness. She knew only how to recognize the scarcity of money and the fear and bitterness that lack created in the lives woven around hers.

Grappling with her wonder about the rich, she concluded that they, the people she would meet in a matter of hours, must be supremely happy. What worries did they have? What scenes of horror had they lived through? None. They probably did not even know places like Margaret's, factories like Mr. Kalish's, and tenement flats like her own existed in the same city only blocks from their castles. Perhaps because they had never clawed against the staggering forces of life, they would be kind. She prayed they would be.

The pounding at the door startled the girl and she stood up.

"Let me in, you hear. Now. Open up."

It was a man's voice, gruff and slurred. Louise waited, hoping he would go away. He must have the wrong room. The door rattled and looked as if it might give way to the man's beating against it. Louise moved to the side against the wall, her hands clenched into fists, ready to strike the intruder if he broke through. Suddenly, the noise stopped, and the girl breathed deeply. Then she heard a key unlocking the door and watched as the knob revolved. The figure who stood in the doorway was tall, thin, dressed in a dark cloak and black silk top hat which he removed and threw on the bed.

"Well," he said, weaving as he neared the bed, "well, I guess you couldn't get the door open, and she had to let me in, insisted on this room." So, Margaret had turned the key.

The man's bearded face was ashen; his nose, straight and wide; his jaws, square; his eyes, black—as dark as his thick hair— and they were bloodshot from his drinking, she imagined.

Bracing herself against the wall near the door, Louise trembled as the man stared at her while he removed his cloak, jacket, and vest.

"Well, I'm here for some affection. Let's get on with some of it, huh? What are you, a new girl here? Guess so. Very young, aren't you? Virgin? No. No virgins in this place. Well, come over here so I can see your face better. Come on. What is this? Come here," he demanded.

The stranger moved toward Louise, grabbing one of her hands, pulling her to him. Crushing her, he slid his drooling mouth all over her face, stopping at her lips. She could not breathe, and when she gasped for air, he shoved his huge tongue in between her teeth. She bit at his tongue with such force she could taste his blood.

Savagely, he threw the girl on the bed, falling on top of her, ripping at the top of her dress. His hands and mouth consumed her. She could feel her soul being torn apart.

When he stopped, fumbling to remove his trousers, Louise knew she was going to die from his attack. With all her strength, she sprang up on the bed and kicked the heel of her shoe into his crotch, feeling the weight of his hardened penis as she made her strike.

Louise leapt forward, her body hitting the door. It flew open.

She heard the man's yelps as she ran down the stairs crowded with shouting, drunken men and women. One flight down and one to go.

"Hey, you," cried a male voice. "You little girl, running to something better than me?"

"Come here, you little whore, and get your ass in my bed," yelled another man in her path to the front door. Other men's raunchy cries riveted together her determination and action to escape.

As she climbed over two men who had passed out on the landing just above the first-floor vestibule, a man came running up the stairs, confronted her, and threw a glass of whisky over her head. Pieces of ice lodged in her hair. Shaking her head to loosen the pieces, she jumped down the last steps past more men and women sitting on the steps, falling cat-like on her hands and feet.

Finally, the vestibule. No sign of Margaret. The door. I must get my hands on the door. Just as she reached for the big, shiny brass knob, a hand seized her arm. She was frozen, afraid to look at the face. It was a man, another stranger, who tried to drag her back toward the parlor. She pulled hard, fiercely, at last breaking away, reaching the door.

"Come back, damn it. I won't eat you," the man's voice followed her onto the stone steps of the house and out into the street.

Louise had escaped from Margaret Dugal's. She kept running until she was breathing so hard she knew she must stop or collapse. Her heart pounded so fast that she was sure it would jump out of her body.

With her hands held to her chest, leaning against the side of a building facing a narrow alley, she looked all around. Men walking with their ladies, carriages drawn by horses, a few automobiles.

Dark clouds shadowed the moon; a heavy humidity coated the night with a sticky mist. Horses' hoofs clopped, striking hollow notes on the street cobblestones. One of the animals excreted waste just steps away from her, and the odor filled her nostrils for an instant. But even this was better than the smell of the man who had tried to rape her. He had been chewing tobacco, and the stench clung to his clothes and body. And now to hers. His breath had tasted like whisky. His face crowded her thoughts. What a nightmarish ghoul.

Margaret had not confronted Louise when she opened the door for that hideous lowlife. *She never expected me to fight him off, and she never dreamed I would be able to break away from her prison,* Louise consoled herself.

When traffic grew heavy, Louise darted to a nearby store doorway and slumped down to rest. Her hunger and weakness were catching up with her. What time was it? Too early to arrive at the Flagler house, wasn't it?

Lights shone in the flats above the stores across the street, and silhouettes of the figures inside moved against the light brown shades pulled down for the night. I can't stay here. Suppose a policeman comes by. What would I tell him? Glancing at her torn sleeves, bodice and skirt, she knew that any officer would assume she was a prostitute who had been beaten up. If she folded her arms and walked with her head down, no one might notice. She would walk close to the buildings, seeking refuge here and there along the way.

"Viva, America!" cried the driver of a wagon in the middle of the street. He was followed by a motor car carrying a man and woman. Vehicles thinned out as she made her way toward Fifty-Fourth Street. Even the delivery men are not out in force, and even if they were, I have no money. Her coins and few belongings were left back at Margaret's—forever. Except the cross which she carried in a pocket.

"Hey, girlie, what are you doing over there?" a humped-over old woman called to her as she braced herself against a storefront door. The woman carried a large straw basket, its handle slid over her arm.

Louise shook. "Nothing."

"They why are you hiding there? Come out on the sidewalk where I can see you." Squinting at the girl, the woman moved closer. "I don't know you. I know most of the girls around here. The ones that walk the streets. I'd say you're too young to be walking the streets. Eh?"

"I'm, I'm going up town. I'm not walking the streets."

"That's what they all say…when they start. Cold feet—they get cold feet at first. I can tell you've got cold feet. Want something to warm you up?" Reaching into her basket, she produced a glass bottle, twisted off the cap with her teeth and held the bottle up to her lips. She guzzled the contents and then held the container out to Louise.

"No, no. No thank you. I don't want any," Louise said, pushing the old woman's hand away from her.

"Come on, take some, my little friend, or I'll tell the police about you."

The woman stood, barring Louise, her arms stretched to either side of the store entrance. When the girl tried to leave, the old woman dropped her basket, applying all her weight to blocking Louise.

"How about some money for an old lady? I know you got money. All you girls have got money."

"No, I don't have any," Louise said. "Look at me. I've been beaten. They took all my money. I don't have any."

The old woman cackled, showing jagged teeth. "Give me your money, and you can go any place. No money? You got shoes. Take off your shoes. Give 'em to me. I've killed girls for less than their shoes. Give 'em here to me."

Louise charged against the old woman, knocking her down. Bolting around a corner, she heard a shrill whistle. Then, silence. The whistle sounded again. The police were after her for hitting the old woman. Down a dark street, around a corner and another, the girl flew—into an alley overflowing with garbage cans and into a doorway with a lighted window to one side. There were horses again. Closer and closer. No, moving away. Where was she now? Fifty-Fourth Street might just as well be a million miles away. A big cat brushed against Louise as she stood panting in a doorway in the alley. The animal was so lucky to be free and fat and belong somewhere. Or was it, too, chasing around in the middle of the night trying to find shelter?

When the world around her was still again, Louise moved slowly into the alleyway, following a shaft of moonlight into the main street.

A sign told her she was at Twenty-Fifth and Fifth Avenue. There were more carriages on the avenue and more people walking. An ice wagon, a milk truck—if only one of them would pass. The men and women who strode past Louise glimpsed at her, but the moon slid behind clouds again, and the street lights were dim so that no one seemed to get a good look at the tattered girl. She did not want to walk too fast—she was sure to attract attention. So she slowed her pace to that of the strollers. Two, four, five, eight blocks. Each block stretched longer, longer.

When she reached Thirtieth Street, she had to stop, to find a recessed storefront for a minute. Ah, even better, there was an alcove with ledges for sitting just inside. Dark, thank goodness. There were no lights in the house that this piece of privacy fronted. The street was deserted. Then she heard rattling noises moving her way. It was a delivery wagon. Peering out of the alcove, she could see a man hauling large cans up to a building opposite her. Must be a restaurant, Louise thought. The vehicle stopped again, and the driver removed more cans and in seconds went back to the wagon and bridled his horses along, closer to where the girl waited. When he made his stop at the building next to her, Louise walked toward him.

"Mister, I wondered if you were going as far up as Fifty-Fourth Street on Fifth Avenue."

"Not my territory," the man said, casting a look at her.

"Oh, how far up do you go then?"

"I'm going downtown to Washington Square. Other wagons'll be along any minute," he said, pausing. "'Course, I could give you a ride. A little way up."

"Thank you," she said, relieved by his offer.

The girl climbed into an open front seat. Reins in hand, the driver directed the two horses around the corner and up the avenue. At Thirty-Fifth, he turned and pulled back on the straps.

His wagon was fully off the street and in a park under a clump of tall trees.

"Why did we stop here," Louise asked.

Dismounting and tying the reins to a tree, he called back to her, "I usually take a break on my run. Get off and rest a minute. Come over here." He was standing, one hand on the trunk of a huge tree when she reached him.

"Where you been tonight, little lady?" he asked, looking at her clothes.

"I'm going uptown to a job, and I fell down on my way."

"Sure," he said, his eyes searching her body. She wished someone else were around. There was no one in the park, no one at all in view anywhere.

"Where are you going this time of the morning to work?"

"Uptown, as I said. Fifty-Fourth and Fifth Avenue."

"Millionaires live up there. What're you going to do around there?"

"Work in a house."

Why was he so interested?

"You got a few bits of change to give me for this ride? Fifteen blocks out of my way, you know."

"I don't...I lost..."

"Well, you have to give me something for my time and the ride. A girl like you...well, you got plenty to give, I'll bet."

"No..."

When she started to run, the short, fat driver came after her, squeezing her arm and mashing her hands in his.

"Whores like you don't get up this way at this time of the morning much. And I sure as hell don't have the time or money to trade with you downtown. Steal from your madam or one of the men? That's what I'll bet. I want to see how you girls operate..."

Struggling with him, Louise kicked at his middle, but he drew back that part of his body every time she tried to stop him with her shoes.

"Yeah, nice and saucy, aren't you? You want a ride, you'll pay me."

Pushing her in the direction of the milk wagon, the man faltered for an instant, losing his balance, shoving her into the wet grass. When he reached for the back slats of the wagon for support, he missed, striking a metal can which fell over and splashed milk on both him and Louise. While he wiped the milk off his arms and face, Louise started to run, but he caught her by her heel, pulling off one of her shoes. With both arms he dived for her feet, grabbed them, and slid her body to him over the dewy, milk-stained grass. This time her strength was sapped. He flung her skirt over her face, tearing her pants down so that she could feel the warm air on her belly. His flesh was suddenly all over her, her legs were thrown apart, and complete blackness flooded her mind. With her last drop of energy, she pushed at his chest and then twisted, finally rocking them both from side to side.

"Help me! Help me! Somebody, help me," Louise screamed.

Her attacker covered her mouth with his hand. Louise could feel his stiff penis on her legs...

"Hey! What are you doing there? Get up, I say," a strong, loud voice bellowed across the park. A circle of light flashed onto the attacker's face, flooding the lines and seams of his skin and his savage, crazed eyes. A quivering sensation raced over Louise. The driver tumbled over and fell by her side.

A tall, heavyset policeman stood over them, aiming his light at the driver's eyes, then hers.

"I should take you both in." The officer stared at the girl.

"I was just trying to get a ride uptown and this man..."

"She's a liar. She's a whore out on the street, and she was working my route. So…I'm a man. I'm alone and I picked her up."

"How old are you, girl?" the officer asked. He moved his light closer to her face. "You can't be over 15, and you, you must be old enough to be her father. Get on that wagon. I don't want to see the likes of you around here again. Get…" the officer motioned with his leather-encased club.

"You whore, you…" the driver grumbled, brushing the grass off his shirt and pants. He did not look back at either the girl or the officer but placed the emptied milk containers upright against the flatbed slats of the wagon, untied his horses, and drove away.

"Officer, I am trying to get to Fifty-Fourth Street and Fifth Avenue, the home of a Mr. Flagler."

"At this time of the morning? Then I am John D. Rockefeller, himself. You'd better get home or to the house where you work before I have to take you down to the station house and book you."

"No, no," Louise cried. "It isn't like that at all. Please, please, you've got to believe me. I…I have a job there at that house."

"Yeah, and what kind of job would somebody like you have at a mansion like that?" the officer questioned.

"Sir, I promise you that if I am lying about this, then you can take me to your station house. Please, will you take me uptown?"

The officer laughed. "A member of the New York Police Department taking a girl like you to that fine house? No, but I'll get you back to where it is you belong."

"I don't have a place to go," a crestfallen Louise explained. "You see, my mother died, and I'm locked out of the flat where we lived, but I've been given a job…"

"Have you got letters, papers, something to prove it?"

"No."

"All right, then. You'll have to move on back where you belong."

"Mrs. O'Donnell is the name of the lady in charge of the kitchen, and I am supposed to report to her this very morning. Please, sir." Louise could not help crying, sobbing. The officer had to believe her. He had to. She could not roam the streets any longer, and if she went to the police station, she would be charged with prostitution. That record would follow her forever.

As they stood in the park between day and night, two strangers, Louise realized she was completely dependent on this man's trust.

Was he like all the rest? Was the world made up of Mr. Kalishes, people like the milkman and the old woman, Margaret Dugal, the drunk who had tried to entrap her?

Falling on her knees, Louise put her head down on the ground and reached to touch the officer's shoes.

She glanced up for an instant, searching for his eyes. "You have to believe me. I have no one else on this earth now. No family. No one. Please, help me."

"I've heard everything at least twice, girl, and yes, I've even had women drop before me like you with their sad tales. Okay, you're young…and I got some time. If this maid in the kitchen of this house doesn't know you, you got real problems. Because then you're lying to me on top of soliciting. I don't like anybody who lies to me, and I don't let anybody take advantage of my kindness. So…get up. Let's go."

As she walked beside the policeman who kept his eyes straight ahead and patted his club into his palms now and then, Louise wanted to thank him and make some promise to repay his belief in her, yet she knew that he still had no proof she was telling the truth.

The policeman walked briskly as rays of sunlight began to appear through the wide spaces between the huge stone houses along the avenue. Behind the black wrought iron gates and fences rose structures so tall and solid and ornate that Louise was frightened. Was she still in New York? She had heard about this part of Manhattan, and her mother had promised one day that they would come here. But they never had, and life at this end of the island remained a mystery to Louise. Until now.

"That is the Astor house…and there is the Rockefeller home… if you didn't know."

"I didn't know," Louise replied.

The officer shook his head. "You're going to work at a great house a few blocks away, and you never were around here before?"

"I was sent here by a friend. It was all arranged, sir."

"Sure, sure. It was all arranged."

"I am to go around to the back, the kitchen door, I was told."

"I wasn't planning to take you up to the front entrance, girl." The officer stopped. "Well, there it is, the home of one of the land's richest. And I hear he's getting even richer down in Florida. Take a good look and pray that you get in on your story."

At the service entrance at the rear of the mansion, the policeman rapped at a heavy, wide door with a small glass pane at the top. In a minute, a woman's head appeared at the glass. Opening the door was a woman, with brown hair drawn up tightly and back from her face, with a white apron spread out over a gray uniform.

"Yes, officer, what can I do for you?"

"I have a girl here who says she has a job with you."

"Oh," the woman frowned, looking first at Louise and then back at the policeman.

"It's Mrs. O'Donnell I am to see. Are you…?" Louise asked.

"No, I am not Mrs. O'Donnell. I am her assistant, Mrs. Wooten. She's busy now…but…I'll get her. Wait here."

"Well, at least you know a name," the policeman said, his

arms folded, his eyes set straight ahead waiting for Mrs. O'Donnell to emerge.

Would Mrs. O'Donnell be so horrified when she saw Louise
that she would reject her? She might. Look at me. Ripped, dirty,
one shoe. I look as though I've come from a garbage pail.

"Yes, yes," a pleasant voice preceded a short woman with
gray-blonde hair and a round, soft, pinkish-white face. Her eyes
were a clear, light blue, and her teeth were even and white. "I am
Mrs. O'Donnell," she smiled at the officer.

"This is, uh…" he said, looking down at the girl.

"I am Louise Lambert. Miss Cecilia, Miss Ida Tarbell…"

"Yes, yes, I was expecting you," Mrs. O'Donnell said. "Come
in now. And officer, thank you. Would you like a cup of tea for
your trouble?"

"No ma'am, but thanks," he said. "Well, girl, good luck."

Turning back to the policeman, Louise stretched out her hand
and shook his. "Thank you for believing me. I won't ever forget you."

"Just don't ever go out on the streets at that time of night,
girl…alone. You should know better."

"Yes," Louise said, "it won't happen again."

Chapter 4

Stepping into the long, cream-colored room banked with rows of double windows, Louise was overcome with everything. The kitchen could have held many of her school classrooms. The white enameled cast iron stove covered the length of an entire wall. The ceiling was so high she felt dwarfed when she glanced up. And the light—the tender, yellow morning sunlight—bathed the whole room. The clear glass window panes glistened, and the shiny sides and bottoms of huge copper pots and pans hanging on the walls dazzled her.

Every element vied for her senses. The smell of coffee brewing; bacon crackling, sizzling; people, freshly scrubbed and dressed, bustling, readying a whole new day.

"I said, welcome, Louise...Louise. Did you hear me?" Mrs. O'Donnell said.

"Yes, yes, thank you, Mrs. O'Donnell. I've never been in a...a kitchen like this. It's so big," Louise said, scanning the room again.

"Yes, yes, I suppose. I forget sometimes. Well, come in and let's get you started. First, your uniform and then some breakfast."

Mrs. O'Donnell stopped, looked into the girl's eyes, and put a hand on her shoulder. "Don't be afraid. You're young, and you'll get used to us and this, this large house."

Louise's eyes fell on her torn skirt. "I...I had an accident on the way here, I'm sorry, I...I..."

"Follow me, Louise. You'll meet the whole staff later," Mrs. O'Donnell said, stopping briefly at the white, wooden rectangular table where they were gathering to eat, and leading her past two of four sinks where Mrs. Wooten stood. She sniffed and lowered her eyes when she saw Louise again.

A wide hall led them to a large bathroom with two tubs ringed from the ceiling by white curtains; two sinks; a commode, and shelves stacked with white towels and facecloths.

"Now, when you've finished, put this dress on," Mrs. O'Donnell said. From a closet she had taken a gray dress like her own. "I will pin it to fit for now. Just come back into the kitchen. Everything you need is here. I didn't see your bag...and shoes...we'll find a pair to fit you."

"No, I don't have a bag, Mrs. O'Donnell."

"Well, no matter. Here," she said, reaching back into a closet, "are fresh underthings, and later I'll see that you get more."

Submerged in a full tub of hot water, Louise spoke aloud, "At last, I am safe for awhile. This is not real. All of this is a wonderful dream, and I hope I never wake up. Oh, Mama, if only you could be here, too."

"Well, you're the second Louise we've had in this house," Mrs. O'Donnell greeted her in the kitchen. "Miss Jenny Louise, Mr. Flagler's daughter, was taken from us just nine years ago. She and the new baby girl..."

"Coincidence, sheer coincidence. Don't let it put things in your head, Louise," Mrs. Wooten broke in. "Besides, the Flaglers had a Carrie, lost her at three. We have a Carrie here."

"Mrs. Wooten, what things to say to a new staff member. Never mind." Mrs. O'Donnell smiled. "Come here, girl. Let's fit this uniform to your small frame."

"Hum," Mrs. Wooten said, eyeing Louise from head to foot. The skin of Mrs. Wooten's face was pinched and lined. Her brown eyes struck Louise as raisin-sized dots set in an elongated glob of dough, reminding the girl of a cookie that was taken from the oven too soon. But that was the only resemblance between a cookie and Mrs. Wooten.

As Mrs. O'Donnell fitted her uniform, Louise smelled a scent of violets rising from the woman who knelt before her on the floor. The long sleeves of the dress were soft and smooth on Louise's clean skin. She could have fallen asleep standing there, wrapped in such pleasantries and attention.

Hands on her hips, Mrs. Wooten stood watching as Mrs. O'Donnell gathered the excess at the waist of the skirt, pinning it behind and tying a white apron over the dress.

"I can't see for the life of me why we're hiring more servants with Mr. Flagler in Florida so much," Mrs. Wooten said.

"Mr. Flagler still lives a good part of the year in New York and has offices here, Mrs. Wooten. Why, this very hour he's busy at his desk on Pearl Street. Besides that, Mr. Rockefeller and some of their partners are here. Mr. Flagler's heart may well be on his paradise in Florida, but his oil business is still very important to him."

"Hum, well, I am not in charge, Mrs. O'Donnell. You and Mr. Hurley are, but if I had anything to say..."

"Turn around and let me see," Mrs. O'Donnell said, nodding to Louise. "Now, come to the stove, and we'll get your breakfast."

The cluster of servants, men and women, who were gathered here when Louise arrived, had gone, their breakfast plates stacked on the drainboard where Mrs. Wooten rinsed silver flatware.

Her mouth watering as she watched Mrs. O'Donnell spoon hotcake batter onto a wide, flat griddle on the stove, Louise

wondered why Mrs. Wooten was so disagreeable. She had everything to make her content—a job, a beautiful house to shelter her,
abundant food, and kind people like Mrs. O'Donnell.

"Now," said Mrs. O'Donnell, when she and the girl finished
their bacon and hotcakes—dredged in butter and hot syrup—
and tea, "your job will be to help in the kitchen, peeling vegetables, cleaning up, and assisting whenever there is a need for two
extra hands. You will dress in uniform, keep to the kitchen and
service area mostly unless Mr. Hurley and I need you elsewhere.
Wages are seven dollars a week, room, board, uniforms, and a
day off a week. I'll advance you wages for this week. If you've any
questions, come to me or to Mr. Hurley. He is in charge of the
entire house. I run the kitchen, and Mrs. Wooten is my assistant.
This is all a lot to remember, but you'll manage. Can you read?"

Louise nodded her head in agreement.

"Good. Now, you can prepare all the vegetables we'll need for
our stew. Here," she said, handing the girl a recipe card from her
pocket. "We've a busy day, Louise. So let's get started."

Mrs. O'Donnell selected carrots, white potatoes, and yellow
onions from a layered wire vegetable bin near the stove. Then she
disappeared, returning with a large cut of beef which she placed
on a wooden butchering table in the middle of the kitchen.

Mrs. Wooten moved along the rows of high cabinets with glass
doors, writing on a tablet as she counted the items she surveyed.

"After you finish the lists, Harriett, would you work with
Louise on the stew, and I will begin the tea cakes for Mr. Flagler."

"Who's coming to tea today?" Harriett Wooten asked.

"The doctors again—Shelton and Talcott. Pity Mr. Flagler
and his suffering wife, Miss Alice."

Louise looked up from peeling a large, Irish potato.

"It's nothing new, my girl," Mrs. O'Donnell said. "You may as well know that Mrs. Flagler is quite ill and is in a sanitarium. She has not lived here for three years."

"The truth is she thinks she's marrying the Czar of Russia, and what's more I heard she keeps saying Mr. Flagler is dead. I even heard last week that she's taken to painting her cheeks with red coloring matter that she extracts from yarn and blackens her eyebrows with burnt cork. To top it all off, she's now putting her coffee cream into her hair as a tonic. She's gone stark-raving mad, and sometimes I believe it's his money that's done it."

"Mrs. Wooten, stop it this instant." Mrs. O'Donnell's voice rose. Her eyes and Mrs. Wooten's locked.

"Hum. It's true, young girl. The goings on in this house...I often think there's a curse with all the money."

"I asked you to stop, and if I have to, I will speak to Mr. Hurley about this," Mrs. O'Donnell said.

Louise glanced at Mrs. O'Donnell, who motioned for the girl to come with her.

Walking through the hall from the kitchen, Mrs. O'Donnell shook her head. "You should see the rest of the house, Louise. There are times here when you'll do errands, odds and ends for us."

A small room with a round table was their first stop. "This is sometimes used for breakfast. And in here is the dining room," she went on guiding Louise into an immense rectangular banquet room. Louise gasped. The dark-paneled room overflowed with objects Louise had never even imagined. The high ceiling was a honeycomb of carved cherubs and flowers painted gold. The massive furnishings were lavished with lion heads, more cherubs, more flowers, and upholstered in crimson and olive green velvet. Mrs. O'Donnell pointed out the objects on the side tables and in cabinets—sterling silver punch bowls, champagne buckets, serving pieces. Louise almost slipped on the parquet floor in which she could see her own reflection.

Mrs. O'Donnell moved on through a reception room with marble floors and finally to an ornate iron-and-wood winding staircase.

"And these are the upstairs rooms, the bedroom suites and more," she said in passing. The study where Mr. Flagler worked was filled with hundreds of books on shelves behind glass doors; chairs covered in raised flower tapestries of pink, green, red; small gold-painted chairs; a long wood table; blue and gold enameled urns which were taller than Louise. Every piece of furniture glistened from obvious polishing with a sweet-scented oil.

"And now to your own room, Louise. Come along," Mrs. O'Donnell said, showing the girl to a small cubicle near the kitchen. Like the kitchen, it was painted off-white. Two double windows, with white shades and panels of lace curtains let the morning sun stream in. In a corner there was a washstand with a white crockery basin and a large, cream-colored pitcher. The bedstead was brass and the thick mattress, bare.

"You can make your own bed fresh. Linens are put in your room every other day. Carrie is in charge of house linens. You'll meet her. And Mr. Hurley. Now, that is about everything—except one important matter. Louise, if anyone should ask, tell them you are 16. I know how old you are, but that will be our secret, all right? Mr. Flagler is a fine man, good to us all. He has his problems. And they are exaggerated by some of our staff. Pay no mind to their tales. They just like to carry stories, goodness knows why. Now, we must get back to our chores," Mrs. O'Donnell said.

Louise's morning was filled with peeling and slicing vegetables for the stew, which was to feed both Mr. Flagler and the staff;

washing the big brown crockery mixing bowls; cutting peaches for a tea cake that Mrs. O'Donnell claimed as her specialty.

Mrs. Wooten did not speak to the girl again, but Mr. Hurley and Carrie did as they floated in and out of the huge kitchen.

After lunch, the staff buzzed with the preparation of tea, sandwiches, and cakes for Mr. Flagler's appointment at four. Only Mr. Hurley and Mrs. O'Donnell actually saw Mr. Flagler and his guests, and their faces were expressionless as they returned several times wheeling an ornate brass tea cart from Mr. Flagler's reception room.

After washing the tea dishes, Louise went to her room to make her bed and freshen up before the dinner service began for Mr. Flagler.

Trying to absorb what had accumulated so suddenly in her life, Louise sat on her bed, the smell of fresh linens surrounding her. Here she was, on a beautiful bed in her own room with a door, her own toiletries, a rug on the floor, windows. The promise of a good meal tonight excited her. The world she had left the night before was a nightmare. And this was a fairy tale, set in a palace. How could her life be so awful and so good? She would work hard for Mrs. O'Donnell, do anything she asked and more.

Louise dared not think about tomorrow or leaving this great house or the fears Mrs. Wooten had raised in her. She would not allow herself to listen to Mrs. Wooten's tales. Instead, she would concentrate on Mrs. O'Donnell and Carrie. How beautiful Carrie was with her full head of blonde, up-swept curls. Yes, she liked almost everyone she had met at the Flagler house, even Mr. Hurley, who had only nodded at the girl, but later in the day said he was happy to have her join the staff. Yes, Mrs. Wooten was the only thorn around, and she was not worthy of any more of Louise's thoughts.

Cecilia, what was Cecilia doing now? Surely she wondered if Louise had made her way safely to the Flagler house. If only she could send Cecilia a note. No, she must not create any trace of her or Cecilia's whereabouts that Margaret Dugal could follow. Somehow, she would find a way to reach Cecilia. Perhaps Mrs. O'Donnell could offer her some advice.

At dinner, Louise saw the entire New York City staff of the Flagler house; there were eight counting herself—Mrs. O'Donnell; Mr. Hurley, a thin, balding man whom Louise thought to be at least 60; Mrs. Wooten; Carrie; Alex, the chauffeur, chubby with brown, curly hair, about 25; the two, middle-aged, gray-haired upstairs maids, Mrs. Egan and Mrs. Talmutt. Mr. Hurley sat at the head of the long table in the kitchen with Mrs. O'Donnell opposite him at the other end. After a brief grace said by Mr. Hurley and some chatter among them all about the good taste of the stew, Mrs. Wooten cleared her throat with such force that everyone cast eyes her way.

"I don't want to accuse anyone, mind you, but silver is missing, some cherished family pieces, and I would hope the pieces would reappear and nothing more need be said about this. Otherwise, I would hate to have Mr. Hurley go to Mr. Flagler himself with the shocking, sad news."

"Mrs. Wooten," Mr. Hurley interrupted her and rose, tapping his spoon on his glass of iced tea, "this is not the time nor the place to discuss this. I will speak with you privately after dinner. Now on with our meal."

A silence fell over the table. Louise could feel the blood rushing to her face. Her first day and a theft. Did they all suspect her?

"Don't let it bother you," Carrie whispered to her. "Wooten, the witch. She's always causing trouble. Likes to accuse. Your first day, and you think you're among criminals. She probably just didn't count right or missed the pieces. I don't think she can see. After supper, how about coming to my room? I've got magazines, and we can look at hairstyles."

Eased by Carrie's conversation, Louise ate her stew, followed by a small cake left over from Mr. Flagler's tea. She had never eaten such delicious food. How lucky all of them were to be around this table. Why would anyone want to steal from a man who was so generous, who fed his help so well?

When Louise was leaving the table, Mrs. O'Donnell caught the girl by her hand. "Mr. Flagler wants to see you, Louise. He meets everyone who works in his houses. So in the morning, before he leaves for his summer home in Mamaroneck, we have an appointment."

"Yes, ma'am," Louise said, a lump in her throat and her chest filled with fear. "Ma'am, I…I didn't take the silver. I would never…"

"I don't believe for a minute that you did or would or could, Louise. Go on with you. You just arrived. Don't worry. In the summer after supper we take walks or sit in the servants' parlor. Then when it cools off a bit, we clean up the kitchen. Do as you like now," Mrs. O'Donnell said.

Carrie's room was just around the corner from Louise's and next to the bath which the two girls shared with Mrs. Egan and Mrs. Talmutt.

Carrie Lee Kirkland was a plump girl with rounded, full breasts and hips, a small waist, pink skin, and golden hair. Her eyes were large and green, and Louise counted Carrie as one of the most beautiful girls she has ever seen. Carrie's room, Louise found, was another story. She could not believe Carrie lived in such clutter. Everywhere Louise looked were jars of cosmetics and hair care instruments. Dresses in pastel voile were laid over chairs. Shoes were piled in corners.

"Mrs. Wooten has a fit about my room. But it's my home so I keep it the way I like," she said, closing the door behind them.

Louise sat on the edge of a chair half-filled with underclothes while Carrie looked at herself in her large, oval wall mirror hanging over a table she used as a dresser.

"Now, Louise, you need prettying up a bit. Come over here. In these jars there is sheer magic. We could, uh, do your hair and face, and you'd look like a regular stage star."

"A stage star?"

"Yes, don't you want to look like a star? I want to be a star, myself. You don't think I want to be a maid all my life. Now, you're a natural beauty, but even nature can be helped. Undo your hair. Louise, and let's see what we can do to make you gorgeous."

As Louise began to remove the few pins holding her long hair at the nape of her neck, she wondered what Carrie had in mind. Looking at the array of scissors, hair combs, and hardware she did not know by name, Louise watched Carrie lining up her beauty tools on the dresser as if she were preparing for surgery.

"This," Carrie said, holding up a long-handled metal instrument with a slim, rectangular piece on the end, "is a Sarah Bernhardt waver and curler, and I think you need a bit more curls around your face...like this." Carrie reached for a copy of *American Hairdresser* and showed Louise the cluster of curls worn by the magazine cover girl. "It's blue-black. Your hair is so black it's blue. I've never seen hair like this," she said, as if she were talking to herself. "You need soft waves in the back and I can do those with this." She displayed what she called the Marcel waving iron. "This has been the rage for a long time in Paris, and it just got here to New York. Some waves will make you look more sophisticated. How old are you, anyway?"

"I am 16," Louise answered, looking straight ahead toward the mirror.

"Oh, just two years younger than I am."

As she combed Louise's hair, Carrie chattered endlessly about cosmetics and hairstyles.

"You know," Carrie said, "you've come to a very important house. Mr. Flagler has more money than he and his son and his children will ever be able to use—and he's the best master among all the rich on Fifth Avenue. I ought to know. My mother works for John D. Rockefeller, himself, and my sister is the personal maid of Mrs. William Vanderbilt. They're fair with them—but not like Mr. Flagler. But you have to be good here, too. Honest pay for honest work." She paused, taking Louise's face in her hands. "You don't steal now at all, you hear. Because that's the fastest way out of this house."

"I wouldn't. I wouldn't," Louise said, pulling away from Carrie and standing up. "What makes you think I would?"

Carrie went to her bed and lay down, propping up her chin with her hands, her elbows resting on the end of the bed. "Oh, I didn't say you did or would. I just want to warn you. I didn't accuse you. You can get an awful reputation among these rich people, and then you'd never get a job along Fifth Avenue in one of these big mansions."

Louise could not hold back her tears.

"Louise, I am sorry I hurt your feelings. I just wanted...I was just trying to help. I thought...come here now beside me and sit."

Louise stood for a few minutes, wiping her eyes with her apron. She longed to tell Carrie that she was only 14, that she had come from a part of New York that Carrie could not even imagine. The truth was so simple and so treacherous. If she told her secrets, Mrs. O'Donnell would be in trouble, and she would be back on the streets again. The truth was becoming a luxury, and Louise wondered if she would ever be able to afford it.

As if reading Louise's mind, Carrie stared at the girl. "Where did you come from? How did you get this job? Your mother a maid, too?"

"No, my mother's dead, and a friend of Mrs. O'Donnell recommended me to her. There was a lot of illness, and I lived with relatives most of the time. I was passed around from family to family. My father's dead. I don't remember much at all."

"I'd say there's some French in you with your dark hair. The eyes, I don't know. We English and Irish and Dutch stock all look alike with our white skin and sandy hair, but you, you're a girl apart...yes. Now, let's see if we can make you even more exciting."

"I am to meet Mr. Flagler in the morning so I want to look my best," Louise said, wondering where those words had come from. She did not realize she felt any particular way about her appearance for Mr. Flagler...until now.

"Oh, you are. Well, he's a fine gentleman and will be cordial to you. You don't want a hairstyle that will startle him. He's been startled enough already by the women in his life. That wife of his, the redhead, Alice. With all her money, they can't help her. Money, clothes, houses, sailing craft. They even named a yacht after her—they call it *Alicia*."

"Do they have any children here?"

"Mr. Flagler had children when he was young with the first Mrs. Flagler, Mary, I am told. They had Jennie Louise, and she passed away and the daughter, only a baby, died, too. And do you know what? There was a little girl in the household named Carrie. She died long before I knew Mr. Flagler—in the middle of the century—and she went at the age of three. Mary Flagler died many years ago, too, in 1881 I think. And they had a son, Harry, who is now 28. He's in and out of the house. He and Mr. Flagler don't get on. Mr. Flagler married Miss Ida Alice soon after his wife died. She was his wife's nurse. Little did he know what he was getting himself into. Sometimes I think that's why he's so busy in Florida. Why, he's making the whole state a European resort with lavish hotels and his railroads."

"Is he moving to Florida?"

"Moving? Well, he spends time in Florida, the winters. Summers in Mamaroneck at his big house there, and it's full of servants, too. Then he's here two days a week or so in the summer. The rich go around so much. They have lots of houses. And he can be in Florida in a few days from here. He has a fancy rail car that whisks him down there. It's a regular house on wheels—with a kitchen, beds, a parlor."

Imagine. Your own rail car. Louise has never even been inside a railroad car and to own a whole car and a railroad—Louise could not fathom such belongings.

"I wouldn't mind if he closed this house, though. I'm going on the stage one day. I am going to be a famous actress. I can't be tucked away in a big house like this all my life. It's not my house. But maybe I can catch me a millionaire when I appear on the stage, and he will build me a castle like this."

"I've never been near the stage."

"Well, one day you'll go, and you'll sit in the front row, and you'll see me dancing and acting up there behind the lights."

"Why do you want to go on the stage?"

"Because, silly girl, you make lots of money in the theater, and everyone applauds you. People idolize you. You're famous. Even with Mr. Flagler's money, there's not a crowd clapping for him. He's not world famous. But you take Sarah Bernhardt. She's old now, but everyone knows her. She's French, too. Why, they even named this hair waver after her. They haven't named anything after Mr. Rockefeller or Mr. Flagler yet. Not even Standard Oil and it's theirs. I always thought they should call it Rockefeller Oil or Flagler Oil— you know, something that tells people they are the owners."

"I suppose that's right," Louise said. She had never heard of Mr. Flagler until yesterday, but then it really did not matter. Look what he had. Everything. Yet he did seem to have troubles with all his money—it was a great pity. But then she had no money, her mother had had no money, and look at their lives. Perhaps vast wealth or deep lack of it had nothing to do with the course of one's life. Or everything.

"Well, now you know all about Mr. Flagler. On your day off I'll show you the other houses around here on this avenue. Some of them are much bigger and more elaborate than Mr. Flagler's. Now, leave your hair the way I've fixed it, all right? And don't mess it up sleeping. Sit up on your pillow if you have to. Keep it smooth. You want to look perfect for Mr. Flagler," Carrie said, finishing with her irons and waver. "We won't put anything on your face this time."

When Louise returned to the kitchen, Mrs. O'Donnell was waiting for her. "I see you've been visiting with Carrie, our resident hairdresser. It looks nice," she said, patting the girl's head. "All the pots need scrubbing and the dishes washing. Let's see how you do alone tonight. I will be in the parlor if you need me. You know where all the cleansers are."

When Louise looked at the mountain of pots and stacks of dishes, she was not sure she would ever be able to finish them. Still, she told herself, she must, and every one of the pieces must be spotless, shining, perfect.

When she was back in her room, Louise collapsed on her bed. Sure her arms had turned to wood, she held one up in the air—it fell back on the bed, numbed. The muscles in her legs pulled and twinged. Her head floated from yesterday to today, to her mother, to Margaret Dugal, to Cecilia, to Carrie. Their faces paraded before her, talking to her individually, then joining their voices in a chaotic chorus. Too much had happened to her in too short a time, and her body and mind could not digest it all.

She could not crowd Mr. Flagler into her head but she must. He had to be uppermost in her thoughts. What would happen to her if he did not like her looks? The hairdo that Carrie created? Her hair was all wrong. Too many pronounced waves and too heavy a mound of hair topping her face. If she changed it, combed it all out, Carrie would probably never forgive her, and she needed her friendship. Louise wanted everyone here to like her.

When Louise was crossing the ledge from wakefulness to that well of sleep she longed for, she heard a pounding at her door. Drowsily she rose, asking who was there. A powerful woman's voice answered. Louise quickly opened the door and saw in a dim hall light the sour face of Mrs. Harriett Wooten.

"I want to come in, Miss Louise Lambert. I have something to say to you."

"Yes, ma'am," Louise said, looking down at her reddened hands which started to shake.

"Now, where is the silver? It's got to be in this room," Mrs. Wooten said, jerking her head from side to side, speculating at the possible hiding places Louise could have chosen to conceal her ill-acquired treasures.

"I took nothing, Mrs. Wooten. I don't even know what silver you're talking about."

"Hum, well, you're not so innocent or so young in the ways

of the world. You can't fool a woman of my experience. Not for an instant. I have had a talk with Mr. Hurley and told him of my suspicions about you."

"No, no. I didn't take it, Mrs. Wooten," Louise heard herself shouting. "Stop it. Stop it. You have no right to accuse me. Look, look around this room right now. You won't find anything."

"I don't know why Mrs. O'Donnell has such a soft heart. She's a fool…"

"Am I, Mrs. Wooten?" Mrs. O'Donnell said, her voice coming from the open doorway to Louise's room.

"You startled me, Mrs. O'Donnell. I didn't hear you…"

"Of course you didn't, but I heard this girl's cries all the way down the hall. Exactly what is this all about?"

Mrs. O'Donnell wore a long nightshirt, and her hair was braided and pinned atop her head.

Afraid to speak, Louise stood watching the two women.

"Go to your room, Mrs. Wooten, and leave this girl alone."

"Yes, yes, I'll go, Mrs. O'Donnell, but I think you'll find this wench is a thief. That you've made a mistake by letting her come into a house as grand as this one. You'll regret it." She turned to Louise, "You see, I am responsible for the silver and the other items of value here, and I have to explain missing pieces. We've have very little thievery until now…"

"Go, Mrs. Wooten. Now," Mrs. O'Donnell demanded.

After Mrs. Wooten left in a huff, Mrs. O'Donnell sat down in one of the two upholstered chairs in Louise's room. Rubbing a hand across her forehead as if she felt deep despair, Mrs. O'Donnell looked straight ahead as if her mind were far away.

"I don't know sometimes. I just don't know about her. Louise, you should understand that Mrs. Wooten is quite a…cunning woman. She's obsessed with running this house one day over me and over Mr. Hurley. She constantly tries to prove my weak-nesses...and yes, I have them. I don't believe giving you this job was a weakness...but well, she would like it to look that way. Now this silver incident. I think we'll find the silver, all of it. Don't let her scare you. Try to forget about this horrible night and get some rest. Don't let Mrs. Wooten know too much about you, Louise. My best advice to you is to avoid her as much as possible."

"I'm sorry I have brought you so much unhappiness, Mrs. O'Donnell. I would never..."

"You haven't brought me anything but perhaps a little light. A chance to help a young, stranded girl. People have helped me all along the way, and my life has not been easy, either. The Mrs. Wootens of the world are always with us...ugh, ugh, get me water, Louise, quickly, a glass of water from the kitchen..." Mrs. O'Donnell clutched her chest.

Louise flew from her room and was back in seconds, finding Mrs. O'Donnell with her head bent down between her knees. Louise leaned over, and Mrs. O'Donnell took the water and held her head back against the top of the chair.

"It's just a little bit of indigestion," she told the girl. "I have it sometimes. Water helps me."

Louise's heart raced wildly. If anything happened to Mrs. O'Donnell, her life at the Flagler house would be over. That future was too awful to picture. She tried to stop such thoughts from forming. After Mrs. O'Donnell rested for awhile, Louise walked her back to her own room, turned her bed covers down, and saw that she was secured for the night.

At least, Louise hoped so.

Chapter 5

As Louise lay in her bed crying—she knew from exhaustion—the shock of her new life and Mrs. Wooten's charge against her as well as Mrs. O'Donnell's frightening illness crowded her thinking. Louise fought to think of something that would lift her from the cavern of fears building within her. She pictured this massive, imposing building that housed her, how it sat like a fortress in the night protecting her, and she held tightly to that image as she drifted off to a deep sleep. The tears finally stopped, and she breathed a final sigh for the night.

When she met Mrs. O'Donnell in the morning in the kitchen, the woman glanced at her, smiled, and patted the girl's face, shaking her head knowingly. She knew, didn't she, that Louise had cried most of the night. Mrs. O'Donnell seemed to know everything.

"Come," Mrs. O'Donnell said, "we have our appointment."

Henry Flagler stood before open double windows flanked by velvet draperies. He held a piece of paper in one hand and rubbed a gold chain on his vest with the other as Louise entered his library. She stood erectly, hands folded before her, behind Mrs. O'Donnell.

"Mr. Flagler, this is our new helper, Louise Lambert." Mrs. O'Donnell turned, and with an arm, brought the girl forward to her side.

He did not seem an old man, as Louise imagined him. He was not tall and frightening as she thought he would be. His cheeks were flushed, his gray-blue eyes were bright, and his hair was sprinkled with silver flecks. His upper lip was concealed under a heavy mustache.

"Good morning," he said in a deep and powerful voice. "Well," he went on, looking at his gold watch, winding its stem, and returning it to a front waist pocket, "so you are new to our house. You could not ask for a finer teacher than Mrs. O'Donnell."

"I told you, Mr. Flagler, that Louise's mother passed away only this week."

"Yes, yes," he said, his eyes growing somber as he looked at Louise. Her heart pounded, and she knew her face must be scarlet. "I am sorry to hear it. I left home before I was your age, but I still had my family. I am sorry Louise," he said, seating himself at his desk. "But don't let your early lot in life scare you or dampen you for the rest of your years. My," he said, looking up at the girl, "your life is just beginning and today, to be young today, with the automobile, with this country opening up, with life bursting all around us, well, life, my girl, is just dawning for you. And in this country, you can have just about anything you dream. But I'd be careful what I dreamed. Dreams have a way of coming true," he said, his voice trailing off, his eyes moving toward the windows near his desk. "Good luck, young lady, and may you find this a good house for you."

"I...I know I will," Louise said. "Thank you, Mr. Flagler." If only Mrs. Wooten would find the silver, then it would be good, everything would be perfect.

"A brilliant, good man. He is so very kind. Why, you know, Louise, after you're here a few months, you have the chance to take part of your pay in Standard Oil stock. I do. I have done this for years."

"I don't understand stock, Mrs. O'Donnell," Louise said when they were at work alone in the kitchen.

"It's shares, ownership—small though mine is—in Mr. Flagler's company. I don't have to tell you how successful Mr. Flagler's Standard Oil is or how rich he is. There are books on the Standard. After Mr. Flagler leaves, I'll get one for you. Are you a good reader?"

"I was one of the first-row students at school."

"Then you can probably teach me a thing or two, Louise. Yes, I'll get you a book on oil and then some more from the library. Mr. Flagler does not mind if we take good care of his books and return them promptly.

Speaking of books, Miss Tarbell, the writer from *McClure's Magazine,* is coming here this very afternoon," Mrs. O'Donnell said, checking a food order list. "I'm proud to say that we are both from Titusville, where the very first oil well was put in by Colonel Drake back in 1859. My father worked for the colonel, and Ida's family worked in the Pennsylvania oil fields, oh, for many, many years. She has lived in Paris and written many stories, the life of Napoleon for *McClure's,* but that was back in 1894, and you would not know...and another on Mr. Lincoln. Why, *McClure's* has wonderful stories by...um...Conan Doyle and Mr. Kipling and Robert Louis Stevenson. Miss Tarbell knows all the big writers. Well, my eyes are a bit strained, you know. It's hard for me to read up close. Anyway, that's the lady who's visiting," she said, glancing at the large clock over the stove.

"Can I meet her, Mrs. O'Donnell?"

"Why, my yes, yes, of course. She wants to see you."

"Since it was Miss Tarbell who arranged for me to be here…I'd like to thank her."

"I might tell you that Mrs. Wooten doesn't take to Miss Ida at all. In fact," she whispered, "the story is a long one. You see Ida was born only a very few miles from Colonel Drake's first well. She grew up in the fields. Her father always had the smell of oil about him, always had the black ooze on his feet when he came into our house, I remember. Ida knows many of the men and their small companies that Mr. Rockefeller and Mr. Flagler have taken over with their big trust. Her brother works for one of the few companies that's been able to make it on its own, independent of the trust.

"Mrs. Wooten thinks Ida's got a war going on in her head against the trust. You see, none of the people in Titusville or in most of Pennsylvania like what Mr. Rockefeller's done in tying every line and company together. My own brother's over in the fields, and he once tried to start his own company He says things are not bad for him now. Mrs. Wooten's brother works in the fields, too. He was hurt on a rig, and the Standard keeps him on a salary anyway. Sometimes I think she thinks the Standard's a god. Bless Mr. Flagler, but the Standard's just not a god to me or Miss Tarbell. All this is to say I try to have Miss Tarbell here when Mrs. Wooten has her day off. They just don't get on at all."

Ida Tarbell came into the house by the service entrance and made herself at home over a cup of tea at the kitchen table. While she was not a pretty woman, there was something in her manner of quiet confidence that aroused in Louise an immediate respect. The proportions of her features were all wrong. Her eyes were set too close together, her nose was too long and wide, and her hairline peaked unattractively. It was her hands, with their long, tapered fingers, her impressive height, and imposing carriage that Louise liked.

Ida Tarbell smiled at the girl during her conversation with Mrs. O'Donnell, a smile that seemed real, honest, and without any motive. Yes, she liked this tall, handsome woman in her plain, green-striped dress.

"You are a good reader, Mrs. O'Donnell tells me," Ida Tarbell said.

"I like to read…"

"I shall see that you get *McClure's*. Then I would like to lend you some of my books, some of those I read when I was about your age. I'll have them sent over to Mrs. O'Donnell."

"Thank you, Miss Tarbell," Louise said, turning back to washing vegetables in the sink.

"I wish you would get to a doctor with those chest pains, Mrs. O'Donnell. I don't like the sound of what happened to you," Miss Tarbell said.

"Oh, it's nothing, Ida. Indigestion, that's all."

"You will see Doctor Trent, my doctor, here in the city. I'll expect you to say you've been to him by the next time I come here. That will be in another week."

"Oh, all right," Mrs. O'Donnell gave in. "For you. But it's nothing. How is Mr. McClure?"

"As filled with ideas and drive as he always is. Geniuses such as Mr. McClure are never easy. But I am devoted to him. You know that. Mr. McClure will change the shape of our thinking about many things over the next few years. Nothing is sacred to him. He is not afraid to print the truth about anyone or anything… now I have to go. Miss Louise Lambert is well situated. Louise, I will get word to Cecilia that you are safe here," she said, glancing at the girl.

"I was wondering how I might tell her," Louise said.

"I'll take care of that and the books. I'll get the books over to you. Enjoy them," she said, patting Mrs. O'Donnell's hands.

"You aren't awfully sick, are you, Mrs. O'Donnell? What is wrong?" Louise forced herself to ask when Ida Tarbell left them.

Mrs. O'Donnell sat down again. "I will confess I do get severe pains now and then. I think it's worry, thinking back too far in my memory. I don't know why I'm telling you this. I'm far too talkative today, as if I am letting down all at once. It's not like me," she said, tears forming at the outer corners of her eyes.

"Mrs. O'Donnell, I am sorry. What is it? Can I do anything?"

"No, no, child. It has nothing to do with you. Seeing Ida reminded me, I guess, of my son and husband. Gone now. I don't talk about them much any more."

Putting a hand on Mrs. O'Donnell's shoulder, Louise sat down at the table. Louise was sure later that this small act made Mrs. O'Donnell cry. Louise did not know why she started to cry, too. When Mrs. O'Donnell reached in her pocket for a handkerchief for the girl, they both stopped their tears.

"Tea, let's get us a cup of tea. I want to tell you about my son and my husband. I won't talk a lot. I will just get it out of my system. They died in the oil fields of Titusville during one of the struggles to build the trust. I would not normally talk about this, especially to someone new here. I think sometimes I was hired here when Mr. Flagler realized I was from Titusville. I came to New York right after that. I had no one left in the world. Friends, but no relatives in Pennsylvania. A woman friend here in New York brought me to a fine, big house and taught me household work. That was at the Depew house some years ago. Now I am passing along my trade to you. You're so young. What do you want to do in life? Have you thought about that?"

"I don't know," Louise said, as she watched Mrs. O'Donnell's eyes peer into space as if trying to gaze into infinity and cast the girl's fortune.

"Well, one thing we can think about. If you should have to leave here...I mean if I should get sick, I won't—I am sure I will not—but just in case, you could go down to Florida and work in one of Mr. Flagler's hotels. He has grand hotels in St. Augustine and now in Palm Beach. I've heard the one in Palm Beach—that's an island way down south in Florida—is a dream Mr. Flagler has made come true. I'll write down the name of my friend who's the housekeeper there. I like to be prepared. But dismiss all that I've told you. I've talked too much today. Let's get to work now."

It was only a few days after Louise met Ida Tarbell that the writer's promised books arrived for Louise. Mrs. Wooten received the box and insisted on Louise's opening it while she stood eyeing a volume of Shakespeare's plays and sonnets, essays by Bacon and Aristotle, Milton's *Paradise Lost*, and assorted copies of the latest editions of *McClure's Magazine* containing editorial sketches of Theodore Roosevelt and J. P. Morgan.

"Rubbish, rubbish. Look at the pages, yellowed, old. The bindings are crumbling apart. Who'd send these to anybody. Who sent them to you?" Mrs. Wooten said.

"A friend of..." Louise remembered Mrs. O'Donnell's warning about Mrs. Wooten's feelings toward Ida Tarbell.

"That Tarbell creature. She sent 'em, didn't she? If you're smart, you'll stay away from the likes of her. She's a troublemaker, she is." Mrs. Wooten scowled.

"You're just jealous because nobody sent you some presents, Mrs. Wooten," Carrie said, kneeling to look at the box on the floor of the kitchen. "I'd like to take this one to my room. Shake-speare. Could I borrow it, Louise?"

"Yes," Louise said, intrigued with her new role as guardian of Ida Tarbell's books.

"You'd better clean up that pigsty before you add anything else to it, Miss Carrie Careless," Mrs. Wooten said.

At that comment, Carrie faced Mrs. Wooten head on. "Oh, go look for that missing silver of yours—that you were so ably in charge of."

"Ladies, please, stop this arguing this minute," Mrs. O'Donnell said, throwing her arms about like oars, clearing a path into the middle of the kitchen where Carrie, Louise, Alex, and Mrs. Wooten were gathered. "Alex, take Louise with you out to the market. Louise, get a sack of white potatoes from Philip's Grocery. Carrie, to your room. Mrs. Wooten, stay here. When you come back from the grocery, you can take these books to your room, Louise," Mrs. O'Donnell comforted Louise.

Reluctantly, Louise followed Alex out the service door and to the garage behind the house where Mr. Flagler's two-seat Duryea gasoline automobile was kept. Alex's face wore a frozen kind of half-grin, and his narrow eyes showed no degree of pain or pleasure. His gray suit with its double rows of brass buttons was pressed completely free of wrinkles, and he smelled of something citrus. It was a clean, fresh scent, and Louise was keenly aware of it.

Louise had never ridden in an automobile, and she was terri-fied as Alex turned the crank of the car at the head of the engine. The motor sputtered under the chassis, which sat on four huge red wheels as large as those of carriages. Louise shook as the machine vibrated, and when Alex climbed in and took hold of the long steering stick, she wanted to jump out.

"Never been in a motor car before? It won't bite," he said, laughing and backing the car out of the garage. The power of the loud machine seemed enormous, and Alex's handling was masterful as he maneuvered corners, slowed the car, braked, and parked it just in front of Philip's Grocery on West Fifty-Third Street. Alex placed the order for the potatoes with the clerk, and he and Louise stood waiting by glass jars filled with red, yellow, and green jawbreakers, the clear, shiny kind that Louise liked. She yearned for one of them, but she had not even a cent with her, and the candies were a penny for five.

When Alex signed the bill, he shook his head, mumbling, "Mrs. O'Donnell could have phoned for these. Can't understand her sometimes," he said.

"What a house you've come to," Alex said when they were in the car again.

"What do you mean?"

"The old bitch, I mean Wooten. And the sick one, Mrs. O'Donnell. Their lives should be switched. Mrs. Wooten should get the bad end of the carrot. I wish Wooten would move to Florida where we tried to send her. She'll never leave New York. Too many relatives here."

When they were back in the garage, and Louise was climbing out, stepping down on the narrow running board, Alex was quickly by her side, grabbing her arm and holding it in a powerful grip. "I've got something I want to talk to you about. It's the silver," he said in a half-whisper.

"The silver? What do you mean? I didn't take it."

"Mrs. Wooten thinks you did and that's what counts. I've got an answer for you, a way out of all this."

"Louise's heart lurched up, pounding out of control. "How, how can I convince her I didn't steal it?"

"If you're good to me, I can help you in many ways. Your day off is tomorrow. Come around to my place upstairs here, and we'll talk about it."

"No, no, I...on my days off you know I don't go anywhere. I can't see you. I promised Mrs. O'Donnell I would read to her."

"You want Wooten to come after you or not?"

Louise hesitated, looking at Alex's squinting eyes. What could he do to her, here at the Flagler house? "All right, I'll come."

"Make it early," he said, " and don't tell anyone about this. I wouldn't want word to get around that I'm playing favorites. Okay?"

"Okay," she said, not sure at all that she had made the right decision. But what choice did she have? Mrs. Wooten could destroy her life if she told Mr. Flagler that she had stolen on her first day of work. Louise would be fired and sent out alone on the streets again.

The room where Alex lived was a dank cave, so sharply contrasted with the bright yellow morning Louise greeted earlier in her own quarters. The brown shades were drawn down to their limits, and a small, green-shaded light with a brass base set on a plain wood table was the only bright spot in the room. Alex walked from the front door to the table. His curly hair was wet, and he smelled of that same cologne she remembered from yesterday.

"Sit down," he said, lighting a cigarette.

"Here." He offered her a small, straight-backed chair with a flat, wooden seat. "You're tense. Afraid of me?" He laughed, extending his grin so that his straight, white teeth showed almost to his ears. "I won't hurt you. This is only a friendly talk. Remember, you're here because I want to help you."

He disappeared, then came back with three large pieces of gleaming silver—a large bowl, used perhaps, she thought, for vegetables, a bucket which he said was for wine or champagne, and a slender bud vase whose etched flowers were encrusted with pearls. "These are the missing pieces."

Louise gasped.

"Never mind how I got them. I got them. I'm returning them to Mrs. Wooten. They're going to be sent by messenger to Mrs. Wooten so that she won't be able to trace the sender."

"But why...why would you want to do that? I...I don't understand."

"You don't have to understand. You have to be grateful that I recovered these, and I'm clearing your name."

Shaking her head, Louise could not comprehend what was happening. How had he found the silver, and why would he go to so much trouble—for her? "No, no..." she said. He moved toward her, staring down at her. Abruptly, he went to the door and locked it from the inside with a key.

"No, no, no please, whatever you want. I'll give you my wages. I'll give you my pay for the next year, forever. Please," she cried.

"You don't even know what I want, do you, stupid little girl? Come here," he said, holding his arms out to her. When she did not come to him, he walked over to her and put his hands on her shoulders. "I am not an animal but I am a man. A man has certain needs. You're a clean girl, and you're young, and I can help you." He held her so that she could not rise from the chair.

"I will expect you, on your days off, to come here to my apartment and do what I tell you, never to reveal what you do here and not to be very, very stupid and get pregnant. If you do, I will deny ever touching you. If you don't do as I wish, I will expose you as a thief. Everyone will believe me. Not you. This is a bondage forever."

"I don't know anything about men. I...have never..."

"Yes, that's why I want you. Take off your clothes...in the

bathroom, hang them up, and come back and lie on the bed. I'll be waiting for you."

Louise lay in total blackness, the smell of sweat clouded over her. She felt not quite human any more. The weight of his fat body on her and in her, sinking and rising, thrusting into her and withdrawing from her was unbearably sharp. So deep and so concentrated was the pain that she knew she must be near or in hell.

She was not Louise Lambert at this moment, a young girl, or even a human being. She was particles, fragments, nerve endings, bits of flesh scattered in space. She, the whole person, did not exist. Her identity was destroyed in those moments of agony, so hopelessly lost that when Alex had finished with her, the force of his body removed from her, she could not function for a few minutes.

She was a wet, soggy sponge. Between her legs she felt as if she were leaking a jelly-like substance. Her body was rubbery, limp, and as she searched her being to regain some feeling, she could not even locate tears. Spent, yes, she was emptied of all belonging to time and place. And yet she must come back, return to some reference. She must get hold. God. Is there such a thing as God, and if there is, come now, come to me, she found herself whispering as she sat at the end of the bed listening to the shower running. He was washing himself of his savagery. He is a beast. An animal from the jungle. I have no relation to him. He is worse than any vulture she could imagine, she told herself over and over.

Alex did not speak to her as he emerged from the bathroom, and she went in to get her clothes. Later, when she was dressed and leaving, he glanced at her as if he hardly knew her. "Remember next week. Your day off," he said.

In the days following her encounter with Alex, she walked in a haze, mired, defeated, and propelled only by the safety of her rituals—peeling, scraping vegetables; washing, scrubbing pots and pans; reading.

Mrs. O'Donnell knew she was different. Louise could feel her eyes, her reaction, and her discipline to hold back her questions and her sympathy. Louise crept out of her cloak of shame and bewilderment only when she was alone with the books Ida Tarbell had sent her. Only with the yellowed pages, the ragged covers, the beauty and life of printed words could she feel any hope of going on.

She clung not only to Miss Tarbell's classics but ventured enough courage to ask Mrs. O'Donnell if she could borrow some of Mr. Flagler's books. She held them with reverence, reading them with a fervor she did not herself understand. Sewing herself into a web of infinite wisdom, she created a niche for herself that no one could invade. She would learn everything she could; she would devour books, collect information that could never be stolen from her by anyone.

When she lay awake at night thinking of all the knowledge there was in the world, her heart began to beat fast, furiously. There was so little time in her life to spend learning, and the thought that she was just on the threshold of her quest made her spring from her bed some nights to read until dawn.

Would she live long enough to understand everything she needed, to digest every important book, magazine? There would always be more, newer information. Even her youth and eagerness could not keep pace with the masses of new knowledge pouring out every day around the world. But she would take on the challenge—for life.

Between her consuming every printed word in sight, from Washington Irving's *Legend of Sleepy Hollow* to articles in *Scribner's Magazine*—which was delivered to Mr. Flagler—her duties in the kitchen, and her appointments with Alex on her days off, Louise would not allow herself any thought. She would go mad if she doted on the black, abysmal hours Alex forced on her. She was convinced he was sexually warped, insane even, but she never talked about Alex even to Carrie, who usually tried new hairstyles on Louise every night after dinner.

"I suppose you don't like it here now since you've gotten used to it," Carrie said as they sat on Carrie's bed, thumbing through a copy of the *Ladies' Home Journal* Carrie had gotten from a stack of old magazines at the Rockefeller house.

"No, no, I do. I am tired all the time," Louise said, praying Carrie would accept that as an explanation for her lack of spirit.

"I suppose. I'm tired, too. And would you look at Mrs. O'Donnell? There's an exhausted one for you. Well, at least you're filling out..."

"Filling out?"

"Up there, you know, at the top. You're growing up...fast, too."

Louise looked at the bodice of her dress. "I am gaining weight. That's all. It's the regular meals, I guess," she said. But when Louise was back in her room, undressed, she looked at her breasts. They were puffing up, her nipples were large and brown. Her waist was getting thick, too. She was too young to be this fat. She felt of her cheeks as she stared into the mirror. Her face was swollen. Suddenly, she seemed bloated all over. It has to be the food. She would cut down at all meals.

Mrs. O'Donnell did not seem to notice her extra weight nor did Mrs. Wooten, whose eyes never missed a speck of soil or a dropped straight pin. Mrs. Wooten's attempts to ignore Louise sanctioned the fact that she saw her and watched her, although after the silver was recovered and placed back on the shelves where it belonged, Mrs. Wooten eased off in her scrutiny of Louise.

"It's such a mystery about the silver, isn't it, Louise?" Mrs. Wooten said, shaking her head at the girl and then raising her colorless, almost invisible eyebrows at Mrs. O'Donnell.

"Well, you have the silver back. What difference does it make, Mrs. Wooten?" Mrs. O'Donnell questioned.

"Hum," Mrs. Wooten said, "it's quite a feat on someone's part. I am only glad that I did not have to go to Mr. Flagler, especially with his burdens these days."

Mrs. O'Donnell did not answer Mrs. Wooten but glanced at Louise and nodded her head as if she had something to tell the girl.

"What's wrong with Mr. Flagler, Mrs. O'Donnell?" she asked when Mrs. Wooten left.

"His wife again. She is worse. I almost forgot, Louise. Here, this came for you today," she said, taking a white envelope from her apron pocket.

"Who could be sending me anything?" Louise said, her curiosity racing. It was a short note, scribbled almost illegibly on paper with an address in small letters at the top. Saint Luke's Hospital, New York, New York.

Louise, my child,
I am here at Saint Luke's and will be for some time, they
tell me. If you can see me, I will be grateful.
With love,
Cecilia

"Oh, no," the girl cried. "It's Cecilia."

"What, what about Cecilia? Yes, she's the woman who knows Ida. What is it?"

"She must be very sick. I have to go to her."

"Yes, yes, of course you do. Here, may I see the letter?"

What could be wrong with her? Was this a trick of Margaret Dugal's? No, she could not get to Louise at the hospital, could she? She must see Cecilia.

"Go ahead today. I will even have Alex drive you..." Mrs. O'Donnell offered.

"No." Louise found her voice rising.

"But why, Louise? Mr. Flagler isn't here. He's at his summer house and..."

"No," Louise said again. "I will walk. And thank you, Mrs. O'Donnell, for letting me go. I'll make it up. The time. I will make it all up to you."

This was Louise's first trip to a hospital, and the odors of alcohol and the cleaning fluid in the bucket used by an old man mopping the gray tile floor of the waiting area fused together and made her gag. She could not be sick here.

Finally, a nun dressed in a long black habit with a stiffly starched, wide white collar and hood, led her up wide, wood stairs to a floor of wards cordoned into rows by green curtains hung from swinging bars attached to the high ceilings. Huge electric fans stood in the corners of the room, and the air they churned against Louise's damp face felt like a cool breeze off the East River.

"You can stay with Miss Bellini for only five minutes. It is difficult for her to talk," the nun said.

Cecilia lay in a corner space, curtained off so that no other patients could see her. When Louise saw her friend, she thought she knew the reason for the isolation. Cecilia's face was completely bandaged, and only the open spaces defining her mouth and eyes gave Louise any indication that this was Cecilia.

Cecilia's hands reached for Louise's.

"Come," she said, her lips unable to form the words wholly.

Louise was stunned. "What has happened, Cecilia?" The girl's eyes welled with tears, yet she knew she should refrain from bringing Cecilia any added sadness.

"A fight, a terrible fight. It's a wonder I am alive at all," she said, the words coming slowly, deliberately.

"Did she do it, did Margaret do this?"

Cecilia shook her head. "I don't know. I don't remember. I only remember the attack. Don't worry about that."

Cecilia tried to lift her body, could not, and sank back. "I just wanted to know that you're safe, Louise. You are all right?"

"Yes, I am, Cecilia. I am fine. What can I do now, Cecilia? For you?"

"I'll be here for a month. The bruises and cuts are bad, and…I won't be the same, Louise, you know," her eyelids partially closed.

"I'll come every day…"

"No," Cecilia said. "You won't come back here. We're taking a risk with your being here now. Margaret Dugal has her ways of finding out about everything eventually."

"I had to come, Cecilia. How will you get along?"

"I don't know. But don't you worry about it. I think Margaret would butcher you if she knew where you were. Please be careful."

The girl's skin shivered.

"There's such a long story to tell you. I can't now. Someday," Cecilia said, her voice weakening. "You better go home now…I meant what I said about not coming here. I will let you know how I am and when I am ready to leave."

"You must need money…or something."

"I have a little in a bank account. Don't worry about that. Go now, please."

When Louise left the hospital on West Forty-Third Street and Third Avenue, she walked back to the Flagler house, hoping that along the way she would be able to piece together some sense to her life, to Cecilia's future. She knew she had provoked Mrs. Dugal to strike out at Cecilia. The attack was her fault. Otherwise, Cecilia would have explained the details of her tragedy. How could she ever tell Cecilia that, yes, she had saved her from the streets, but that she was a captive, some kind of sexual slave in the Flagler house. There was no one Louise could tell. Her life was an endless nightmare, a cruel maze leading where? She thought of Margaret Dugal's house, and a dark tunnel of horror ran through her mind. No, she would never go back there. But where?

She would have to earn money to help Cecilia. Poor Cecilia. She couldn't go back to Margaret's. Her face might be disfigured for the rest of her life, and she would have to take a job away from the public. In a factory, yes, she might have to work in one if her face did not heal properly. Louise would never let that happen. She was young and strong. There has to be a way I can help her and free myself from Alex. There has to be, she thought, as she walked swiftly toward Fifth Avenue, feeling the frenzied movement of life all around her.

There are thousands of people worse off than I am now. She winced at the old women whose feet were bound in rags for shoes and at children whose outstretched, begging hands were filthy and whose short pants and dresses were torn and patched. They seemed helpless. They were to be pitied. "Not I," she said aloud. "I have a roof over my head and food and a job. And Mr. Flagler. He has risen above it all. He is an island, yes, an island somehow of hope among this, this mass of people. There is a way. There are many, no, hundreds of ways I can help Cecilia. It's just finding the right one, the one that will work best," she kept telling herself until she reached the great stone house she called home.

Chapter 6

"If it makes you feel any better, I will clean my room—but in my own time, you old bat," Carrie screamed, her face crimson as she belted out a counterattack at Mrs. Wooten. Louise, who had just stepped into the kitchen, heard Mrs. Wooten's thrashing of Carrie. Both women were so engrossed in their exchange of fire they ignored her presence.

"Hum, if it pleases me. If it pleases the owner of the house. We're not running a farm here. This is a great and important house, and I said clean up your room. Now."

"You're not my boss, Mrs. Wooten. Mrs. O'Donnell is."

"Well, Mrs. O'Donnell is out, and I am in charge, and I say off to your room this instant."

Carrie turned away, looked at Louise, and sighed. "It is no use," she said.

"And the beer. I can smell it on you from here. You know Mr. Flagler allows no alcohol among us, and you've broken that rule as well as inviting rats into your room."

Carrie's curls had collapsed in the heat of her battle with Mrs. Wooten and the steaming summer kitchen. "It's no good talking with you, you old, old...oh, what's the point of arguing with such a bitch." Carrie stormed off past Mrs. Wooten, whose eyes followed her adversary into the hall.

"I wouldn't advise running after your friend. She's in trouble not only with me but with Mrs. O'Donnell. Drinking beer all afternoon. It's disgusting. Mr. Flagler does not touch alcohol or permit us to drink on these premises. Let that be a lesson to you, Miss Louise," Mrs. Wooten spouted. "And you, where have you been all afternoon?"

"Mrs. O'Donnell said I could go…"

"Hum. I knew nothing about her giving you any permission to leave. Someone should have told me," Mrs. Wooten said, wiping the drainboard of water spots and hanging her cloth in the small closet next to the tall ice box. "Finish cleaning up here. Dinner is light. Cold chicken and salad. Everyone is out…somewhere tonight. Set the table, and you will clean the kitchen alone tonight. That ridiculous girl, Carrie. Drunk. She's a sot. That is certain."

After dinner, Louise found Carrie lying on her bed crying, her room in its usual disarray. "I'm leaving this house. I swear I'm leaving," Carrie sobbed.

"You can't go, Carrie. You just can't."

"That damn Wooten. I hate her, Louise. I despise her. She's always after me. The linens are never clean enough. A spot here, a wrinkle there. My folding is always off, according to her. And the uniforms. Never properly ironed. Look at my hands. Look at my callouses from trying to please her." Carrie held up her palms for Louise to examine. "And what're we doing all this for, anyway? Mr. Flagler is never here. This house is a tomb. It'll be sold one of these days unless Mr. Flagler gets married again and brings life back into these rooms."

"Do you think he'll sell this house soon?"

"Oh, I don't know, Louise," Carrie said, propping herself up against her pillows. "I shouldn't put sad things into your little head. You'd have nowhere to go if you lost this job, would you?"

THE RICHEST WOMAN IN THE WORLD - BOOK ONE 91

"No, I wouldn't. Unless I could get a job in one of Mr. Flagler's hotels down in Florida."

"That's only for wintertime. Nobody stays in those swamps in the summer. I've heard it's a jungle down there. You know, panthers and deadly bugs. Alligators. It's uncivilized."

"Why does Mr. Flagler have hotels there?"

"The sun. Lots of people go there for the warmth and the sun when it's freezing here. He's made it bearable, quite nice in fact, with all of the services and dinners. But beyond the hotels there's nothing. Well, I guess you could get by. But I'm going on the stage for sure now. I am leaving here," Carrie said, with a determination that both excited and frightened Louise.

"And I'm going to make money, lots of money."

"Are you? How?"

"I don't know yet..."

Carrie cast an eye at Louise. "You're pretty enough for the stage, and you could make money there."

"I want so much money, Carrie, that I can erase every pain in my life. I can push back all the tears around me with enough money."

"That's a strange way of putting it. I never heard anyone say that about money. I wonder if anybody ever gets enough money to keep pain away."

"Yes," Louise said. "If I had enough money now, and I had had enough awhile back, I could have kept my mother alive."

"It must have been a terrible illness your mother had. Was she sick a long time?"

"No...but if I had had the money then...it could have been different. Her life...I need money now to help someone else. I have to get lots of it."

"I wish I could tell you how. I never really thought about hordes of money. I don't even care about it. I just want to be an actress. I can take money or leave it. Although it might be nice to have some. Then you take a look at Mr. Flagler…it hasn't brought him much happiness…I think I'd better sleep now, Louise. If Mrs. O'Donnell asks for me, I'm dead to the world, all right?"

Carrie was not at breakfast to hear that Mrs. O'Donnell had visited Dr. Trent, Ida Tarbell's doctor, who warned her that she had a weak heart and that her work in the Flagler house would have to be lessened. Mrs. O'Donnell and Mr. Hurley had already spoken to Mr. Flagler about Mrs. O'Donnell's health. Mrs. O'Donnell would be more of a supervisor from now on, Mr. Hurley said, and would not be involved in the day-to-day operation of the kitchen.

When Carrie learned that the servants would answer more directly to Mrs. Wooten, she balked. "Now I know I won't stay," she told Louise. "Come with me, Louise, before you die in this place. And don't think I don't know what hell you're going through. Old Alex has got to you, hasn't he? I wouldn't be surprised if you're pregnant."

Louise stared at Carrie, trying to accept what she said. "What do you mean? I'm not."

"You're not? Look at you," she said, pushing Louise to the long mirror in her bedroom.

"I can't be. Alex…"

"Don't you feel bad, sick? Well, you look…fat, pregnant. I know the signs. When did you have your period last?"

"I'm late," Louise admitted.

"You're late. Well, I knew something was going on. Why didn't you tell me?"

"He said if I told anyone…he'd have me fired. He'll destroy

me. Please, Carrie, don't…don't tell anybody. How…how did you know?"

"I've seen you go to his place. He almost tricked me once. Oh, Louise, you're so young, and you don't understand the world. You can't stay here."

"Where will you go, Carrie?"

"I'll get a room near a little theater on Forty-Second Street. They're doing a musical there in the fall, and I am going to learn to sing and dance. Have you got any money at all saved?"

"Yes, practically all my wages since I've been here. But I have to use that money…now…"

"What for? Well, maybe you don't want to say. I could let you have some money…but if you stay here your life will be hell, I tell you, with old Wooten and…and Alex."

"What will I do if I am pregnant, Carrie?"

"You'll have to get rid of it."

"Get rid of it, a baby?"

"Do you want a baby, Louise? Can you take care of a baby?"

"No, I can't…"

"A baby could wreck your life. You would certainly be fired by old Wooten if she thought you were pregnant. That's worse than drinking, and I nearly got fired for a few beers."

When she was alone, Louise felt her abdomen. Was it possible she was carrying a new life in her body? What had she done? Why hadn't she run away from Alex? Fear had practically ruined her life. Not only had she defeated herself, she had betrayed everyone—her mother, Cecilia, Mrs. O'Donnell, Ida Tarbell. She could not have a baby. She was only a child herself. She had to grow up, start seeing people for what they were and the world for what it was. Hadn't she been scarred enough to recognize that most men were depraved, unleashed devils out to hurt her, all women, using them for their carnal pleasures? She hated men. She loathed Alex, and right now she could not tolerate herself. How could she possibly help Cecilia if she were pregnant?

What a fool she was!

When her period did not come in the next two weeks, and she could not stand the smell of coffee or bacon, and she began to have dizzy spells, Louise admitted that, yes, she could be pregnant. She dared not say anything to Alex, who, on her days off, went through his usual steps—pulling the shades, making her undress in the bathroom, and lie still while he used her body until he was completely satisfied. It was strange, she thought as she lay on his bed, that he did not suspect he had dropped his seed into her, that there was a union between them.

When she closed her eyes, frozen in her position as he pumped himself up and down on her, she pictured his face reacting to her announcement that she was going to have a baby. Where would his grin go then? Well, he had already said he would deny any contact with her in case she did conceive. And who would believe her if she accused him of raping her, trapping her into this bizarre relationship? He did not connect this, this orgy, with any product remotely human. Birth was only a consequence she had to face. For him there was no responsibility, no tie, nothing. He was sad, dismal, ugly. And she was as pathetic. A child of theirs would be cursed, perhaps, yes, as she herself was damned now.

"You could be pretty, yes, quite pretty," Alex said, when she was dressed. That was the first time he had ever looked at her and seen her. Standing there, watching his eyes feast on her body and her face, she realized something she had never thought of before, ever. A man, any man, is weakened by this sensual, fleeting force that he commits under the trance of his own wild lust. A woman need not be entwined in the act. And her reaction does not matter to the male, for he performs his love act almost by himself. Anyone could lie under him, anyone could be used. Love making—there was no love involved.

How completely different we are, men and women. Is there love between man and woman...no, it can't be. Love does not exist. Oh, but hate does. The kind of hate Carrie feels for Mrs. Wooten and the kind of hate I feel for Alex. Louise had no love to embrace, and so hate would have to motivate her. Now there was no choice.

She knew she was getting hold of her life when she listed in her mind her alternatives for the future. She could tag along with Carrie, blundering into a life she could not even imagine. Carrie's dream could become hers, but she did not feel comfortable about becoming an actress. The world of pretense, of acting, slipping behind the mask of another character, no, that was not for her. No matter how bad her life was, she wanted to live it, to fight, to see what would happen to her, what she could make of herself, her circumstances.

On the other hand, she could stay here in the Flagler house, beholden to Alex and pandering to Mrs. Wooten until Mrs. Wooten discovered she was pregnant. That would bring immediate dismissal. There was a slim chance of going to Florida, at least for the coming winter, to be a maid in one of Mr. Flagler's hotels. After all, Mrs. O'Donnell did give her the name of the housekeeper at the Royal Poinciana Hotel in Palm Beach. She would have to speak to Mrs. O'Donnell about traveling to Florida. Was the offer really open—they had not discussed Palm Beach after that first time.

All of her thoughts were not leading Louise to her one major concern—Cecilia. Her friend had to have help, and help was money, a job, a new start. No matter how proud Cecilia was, she must accept Louise's support. Who, even among her Tammany Hall contacts, would come to Cecilia's rescue if her face was marred for life? At least, Louise knew enough to realize that men did not have time or money for ugly, disfigured women.

Which way should she turn? What road first?

When Carrie appeared at Louise's bedroom door late at night, waking the girl with her banging, Louise was sure Carrie was leaving, and for an instant, in her state of half sleep, pictured herself packing the two dresses Carrie had given her and stealing into the pitch black night.

"Carrie, I beg you. Don't leave here without me. Please…"

"No, no, I'm not going tonight. I will go in my own time. I'm making arrangements. I am not here about myself. It's you," Carrie explained, "I've come to get your life straightened out. I have something that will free you. Tonight. Look, it's a piece of hemlock."

"And what is it for?"

"Oh, Louise, Louise. Don't you know anything? Haven't you heard of women using this to get rid of the fetus, the forming baby inside you?"

Sitting straight up in her bed, the room dark except for the light from the sliver of moon, Louise shook her head slowly. "No, I don't know anything about that," she said, as she looked at the tiny piece of woody substance Carrie held out for her to feel.

"You insert this in your womb and you wait. It's wood, it swells and cuts the fetus loose from you."

"I've never heard of such a thing."

"You'd better use it or you can't come with me, Louise. I can't take a pregnant girl into the theater. You need your health, and you've got to look your best. It's your decision, but you don't have much choice. You'd better hurry. Wooten is beginning to suspect something. She's saying to the others that you're a 'little whore' and that could mean she knows."

"Who did she say that to?"

"The other maids. You know how everyone talks. They couldn't wait to tell me because they knew I'd tell you. You're not the most popular girl in the house, you know. Friend of Mrs. O'Donnell's and friend of Miss Tarbell's, plus you're my friend. Well, what do you say?"

"I don't know, Carrie. I just don't know what to do."

"I know a woman who did this and nothing life-threatening happened. She bled and was sick awhile and that was the end of it. She was fine. You can't go to a doctor to help you. Do what you want. But do something. Do you understand how to use it? Are you sure?"

"Yes, I understand."

"All right. If you need me, I'll be in my room, clearing it so I can get to the bed."

For what seemed a long time after Carrie had gone, Louise sat staring at the moon, listening to the silence of the night. It was good to be alone, not to have voices, thoughts, intrusions bombarding her. What she did would have to be her own decision. This was her body, her future, and she could not satisfy the convictions of any other person. She rubbed the piece of jagged hemlock, imagining that it was already in her body, scraping away life. Her thoughts sickened her. This tiny piece of innocent nature could destroy the most superior creation on earth, a human life. Yet the child she carried could bring lifelong disaster and suffering to Louise and the child.

Walking to her bureau in the dark, Louise opened a lower drawer and wrapped the hemlock in a handkerchief. Closing the drawer, she shook her head, reminding herself that she was simply putting off the decision. She could not face dealing with this tonight.

During the next few weeks, Louise avoided Carrie's questioning glances, losing herself more completely in her reading and reacting to Alex with passive indignation. She did not speak to him at all when she went to his apartment.

Often, she thought that both she and Henry Flagler were afloat on a painted sea. His wife was not getting any better, Mrs. Wooten reported, and he could not, under the laws of New York, obtain a divorce from an insane spouse. Some doctors, said Mrs. Wooten, were sure that Mrs. Flagler would never emerge from the sanitarium, that she was hopelessly insane. Even though Mr. Flagler was in his 60s, he has a life to live, years to use his money to make each day a fantasy. At least Louise was not encumbered. She was free as the wind…except for the baby.

Louise's only responses now were to poor Mrs. O'Donnell who was spending more and more time confined to her room. It was Louise's job to take breakfast and supper trays to Mrs. O'Donnell.

"I can't see for the life of me," Mrs. Wooten said, as Louise returned to the kitchen with the trays from serving Mrs. O'Donnell, "why Mr. Flagler keeps her on here. I am running the house, well, Mr. Hurley and I are. She should go to a hospital where she can be treated. But no, the doctor has to come here to see her. At

Mr. Flagler's expense, too. He's good beyond reason. He is too kind, and she is taking advantage."

"How can you say that, Mrs. Wooten? Mr. Flagler would do the same for you."

"Hum, well, I wouldn't take the charity. I…I just would not."

"I suppose that's easy for you to say. You are so strong now."

"Now…hum. I will always be strong. I can't say as much for you. You're awfully slow for somebody so young. If I had my way, you'd be shipped out of New York on one of them orphan trains that takes children to the Middle West and drops them off to be taken in by strangers. You're too young to be taken into a house like this. No experience. Sometimes…and don't think I couldn't arrange with the Children's Aid Society to do just that to you. So get busy."

"What are these orphan trains? Why do they take children away from New York?"

"Because there's too many homeless urchins on our streets, hungry they are, too. Children nobody wants. Dirty children… filthy…from the immigrants, bastards most of them, produced by starving vagrants. God knows why they keep having children. Stupid people. At least their offspring have a chance. They're taken to farms, mostly as hands. Some live with families, in the same house. And some, I hear, are sold as slaves, auctioned off. Well, why not? Somebody's got to pay for their train fares and their keep until they can get out of New York. You ask too many questions, girl. Get to work now or you will be on a train out of here. You might even be auctioned off. Though I don't know why anybody would pay a cent for you. Get to work now. Polish the silver, the flat pieces."

"But I just did that yesterday, Mrs. Wooten."

"I said polish the silver and after that the marble floors at the entrance of the house. After that, peel the onions, wash the cabbage, and scrub the kitchen floor. I'll show you what work is all about so as you'd be happy to get an orphan train to anywhere."

Chapter 7

"You're not going to get rid of Alex's child, are you? You intend to have the baby, right in your own room, I'll bet, and then steal away into the night…and end up working in one of those factories down in the pits of New York. Or…you might be so shocked by the birth that you'd put the child in a trash can and kill it that way," Carrie said, her eyes boring into Louise's soul.

"No, no, stop it, Carrie. Don't you think I want to do something? But I can't…I can't kill a life that's in me."

"Oh, I lose patience with you, Louise. Well, I did not come here to belabor the question. Your life is your own. And mine is mine. I'm saying good-bye. I found a room—here's the address. If you ever want a job, maybe I could help you out. The trouble with you is you think too much. Maybe those books are doing you a lot of harm. I'm leaving in the morning before breakfast…so this is farewell, Louise," she said, embracing the girl.

"I've got only this to say to you. Wake up, before the world just rolls all over you. Grab hold of life and make it work for you. You know, without me here you won't have anybody. Mrs. O'Donnell is dying by the minute, and then what's to become of you?"

"I may come to you, Carrie. Thank you for this," Louise said, folding the piece of paper bearing Carrie's new address on Forty-Second Street.

"I left a few things in my room for you. Hair curlers, dresses, shoes…"

"Thank you, Carrie. I'm sorry I've disappointed you."

"Don't apologize to me. It's your life."

The house was empty without Carrie. There was no laughter or fighting, only the drudgery of the kitchen. Louise pushed her heavy, increasingly clumsy body through the cleaning, washing, polishing, wiping, peeling, cutting. Carrie was right. She had to act immediately. It was probably too late for the hemlock to work. After all, she was two months pregnant.

When the house was bedded down and all the lights were out, Louise went into the bathroom down the hall. She inserted the hemlock, washing her hands over and over to cleanse them of her act. It was murder she had just committed, her inner voice kept telling her. Screams echoed through her head.

In her room, she lay still on her back, waiting. There was no feeling at first, and then came the sensation of movement in her abdomen, no, lower, in her womb. It was only a tickling at first, then stabbing, excruciating pain consumed her whole body. She wanted to yell to release some of the agony. Holding her hands over her mouth, twisting her body from one side of the bed to the other, she finally kicked her feet into the air, sat up, and fell down again on the bed. She pressed her hands against her ears, then raked her hands through her hair. Her body poured out a hot, feverish sweat. The pain stopped suddenly, and she realized blood was gushing from her womb. It was all over her legs, the bed sheets—thick clots of blood. She could not bear to look as she ripped off the sheets and covered them with a blanket.

She could not stay here. Carrie, she must get to Carrie. The sheets, she could not leave them. Money, Carrie's address. She must have those. And her mother's cross—she had left it in her closet on the top shelf in a small box. She found it and placed it in her dress pocket. Forcing herself to move on a reserve of energy, she reached for fresh underclothing and put it on, rolling the soiled things into the bed linens.

A thin trickle of blood soaked her fresh pants within seconds. She found Carrie's address and from under her mattress she removed a folded newspaper which held her meager savings.

After putting the money into a drawstring cotton bag she had made for a purse, she collected all remnants of her crime and put them in a laundry bag which she carried along.

Her head was so light she felt as if she were being lifted onto a cloud. She saw her room and the street and traffic through a film of gauze. Could she make it to Forty-Second Street? She must take a carriage...yes, there's one.

Carrie's rooming house was a red brick, four-story building wedged between two taller structures. A light in the hallway shone on a row of mailboxes in an alcove. "Carrie Kirkland," Louise read aloud, "Room 314." Gripping the railings leading up to the third floor, Louise climbed each step, every one of them stretching into a mile of pain. She was weaker with every breath.

When Carrie opened the door, Louise managed to say only, "I've done it." Then she collapsed.

When Louise awoke—it seemed days later—she lay in a narrow bed. An old, white-bearded man was leaning over her and shoving a bottle up to her mouth. "Here," he said, touching her mouth with the lip of the bottle. "Take a slug of this." She drank of the amber liquid. Whisky? She shook her head as her body twinged from the sour taste.

"Keep her lying down for a day, maybe longer. I've packed her and that'll need changing. I'll have to come back unless you want to bring her to my place. These pills will keep down the infection," he said.

"Thank you, Will," Carrie said.

The figures before Louise moved under a veil. She knew where she was but...who was this Will?

"My God, Louise. Why did you ever... Well, it doesn't matter now. Rest. Sleep. I'll think of something to tell Mr. Hurley," Carrie said. "Thank God for Will. He was a doctor in the Civil War, believe it or not, tending Confederate soldiers, and he was a Yankee. The Yankees nearly killed him for that, and the government took away his license so now he hangs around the theater, restaurants, helping anybody who needs him. A saint. A drunk one, but a saint. I'm damned lucky to have found him at this hour of the morning."

Louise heard Carrie, but her voice was becoming fainter with each word. She was aware that Carrie was by her side whenever she opened her eyes, feeding her soup, calling the doctor again, changing her bed and her clothes. She even went to the Flagler house with a story to explain Louise's disappearance—which she recounted for Louise.

"They think something's strange but who cares? You still have the job, Mrs. O'Donnell said. I told her you took sick and were afraid to go to Mrs. Wooten. She believed me, I think. Well, maybe she didn't. But the point is you can go back and work. God knows I can't keep you, and I can't get you on at the theater. I may have to go back to being a servant again, too," Carrie said.

"But I thought you were going to learn..."

"It isn't that easy. I can't ask my mother to help me either. She's got all she can handle."

"Then what will you do?"

"Oh, for now get you well enough to take care of yourself. You have to do something to keep Alex away from you, little girl."

"I just can't fight him, Carrie. I'm too weak to think about him. I can't go through this again."

"You're telling me. Doctor Will says you almost died. You lost enough blood to kill a healthy man, he said. Looks like I caused it," Carrie said, casting her eyes down.

"No, no you didn't, Carrie. You saved my life. I won't ever forget that. I know what I have to do now. I must go back to the house and see Mrs. O'Donnell, and then I'll head for Florida. It's almost November and the season will begin soon. I'll get a job in one of the hotels."

"That doesn't sound so bad, does it? I may have to join you one of these days if I can't get a job in a musical. There's always a chance, though, that they'll call me. I have to look on the bright side. I haven't given up my dream. I'll never give it up." Carrie's eyes danced with excitement, and to Louise she was already a star, a great actress. She was electric, strong. Carrie could take the reins in any situation.

When Louise returned to the Flagler house, Mrs. Wooten nodded at her in a preoccupied manner.

"Mrs. O'Donnell is very ill, and the others are on holiday until the end of the month. So that leaves you and Alex and me. Mr. Hurley's sister is sick, and he's away. You got sick at the wrong time, Miss Lambert," she said as she went about her kitchen work. "Get to scrubbing the floors...and take all the bed linens into the laundry room. You'll have all the linens to do now. And not the way Carrie did them either. What a horrible mess she made. I'll show you the proper way, my way."

When Louise visited Mrs. O'Donnell, the woman seemed

only partially aware of her presence at first, and then she whipped into a long, normal conversation, her eyes brightening.

"My heart pumps right sometimes but wrong most of the time, Louise. You look pale yourself. I'm sorry you were ill, too," she said, holding the girl's hands. Even as she lay there, close to the end of her life, Louise thought, she was the picture of kindness. And she was lovely. Her hair was combed and up-swept. She smelled of sweet-scented talc. Mrs. O'Donnell wore her illness with a kind of dignity, and if death came for her now, Louise thought, it would not be an ugly, horrible scene. Mrs. O'Donnell appeared somehow ready, resigned to a peaceful departure.

"I want to go to Florida, Mrs. O'Donnell. I need to..."

"Yes, yes, fine...you know the lady to see. It will be better for you there. And you won't forget to be in touch with Ida, will you? She's come here to see me in the last day or two...I forget...and asked about you. You'll write to her wherever you go?"

"Yes, yes I will, Mrs. O'Donnell."

When she left Mrs. O'Donnell, Louise felt a security she had not experienced many times in her life. She had a destination. She could leave here and go to Florida, and there would be a place for her. Money to make. Money for Cecilia. A new life for them both.

On her day off, Louise did not go to Alex's apartment, and at noon he came for her in the kitchen where she worked alone.

"You had an appointment today, Louise. You didn't forget, did you?" Alex asked, his arms folded, his eyes glued to her as she stood firmly in front of the ovens.

"No, I didn't forget. I'm not going to my appointment any more."

"No?" His face flushed and his half-grin faded, his mouth closing and drooping at the corners.

"No. I have a disease and…"

"What kind of disease?"

"It is a social disease…and the doctor says I can be cured, but…"

"Wait. Stop. Sit down. There at the kitchen table before Mrs. Wooten comes back in here. You have a disease…"

"Then you could have it, too, or maybe you gave it to me."

Alex's face blushed tomato red. "I never gave you any disease… but you…you gave it to me…you little slut…"

"Lower your voice, Alex. If Mrs. Wooten finds out, you could be fired yourself."

"If this is some kind of trick…I'll find out fast enough."

"Do you want the doctor's name I went to?"

"So that's why you were away those days. What did they give you. What kind of medicine?"

"I don't know, but you can't buy it at the pharmacy. Luckily, I had a friend who was able to get me to the right doctor."

"Okay, okay." Abruptly, he arose with a worried, almost tormented expression on his face.

Louise had to hold back her laughter, trapping it in the pit of her stomach. Carrie has the imagination of a novelist. She should be a writer, not an actress. Her scheme had worked. At least for now. Her friend had hit on the one thing that scared and at the same time mystified Alex—Alex so immaculate, so clean, now burdened by the possibility of having syphilis or gonorrhea. He was probably headed for a doctor's office at this minute, and he could not be a doctor who was in any way connected with the Flagler household. The trap was weirdly funny, and Louise felt a deep sense of strength in her ability to carry off the farce.

In the afternoon, after Louise had bathed and put on one of

the long wool dresses Carrie had left for her, she asked to speak with Mrs. Wooten in the kitchen.

"Well, what is it?" Mrs. Wooten questioned, outwardly agitated by the girl's request.

"I...I want to leave and go to Florida..."

"You want to what? Who put you up to this? When I am short-handed as it is, you want to leave and go to Florida. Mrs. O'Donnell planned this. I know she did to make everything harder on me. She's jealous that I am taking her place. No, I won't permit it. I won't let you go. I'll stop you any way I can think of. You're not much, but you're trained now, and I can't be bothered with new people, not now. I know the staffs in Florida. I'll see they don't hire you. I'll see that you're put on a black list. That nobody will hire you down there. Mr. Flagler controls everything in Florida nowadays."

"But Mrs. Wooten...you don't like me."

"The brazen nature of you. No, I don't like you. But that's beside the point in this discussion. You will stay here and do as I say unless you want the orphan train, unless you want the streets."

Would it do any good for her to go back to Mrs. O'Donnell, to ask Mr. Hurley or Mr. Flagler himself? Louise felt trapped again by what lay outside this house if she left without a direction.

In the days and weeks that followed, Louise clung to her books, to her duties at the house, to the short visits she had with Mrs. O'Donnell—who never questioned the fact that Louise did not, after all, go south—and the short notes from Cecilia who was still hospitalized and insisted that Louise not visit her again until she gave her instructions.

Even when the two other maids and Mr. Hurley resumed their jobs, Louise knew not to broach the subject of going to Florida.

Of course, Louise could run away and go to Florida using

another name. No, Carrie told her when she broached the idea. "No one will hire you at a hotel without references. Old Wooten can't last forever. That's your only hope," Carrie said. Louise was not sure Carrie was right.

Mrs. Wooten was surely built of iron ore. She, above everyone Louise knew, seemed to be indestructible. When Louise accepted that Mrs. Wooten did have her chained to her position, Louise decided to make the best of it, obeying the woman, refusing to argue with her or combat her orders and asking only that even more of her salary continue to be held for payment toward Standard Oil stock.

"I don't know how you live with all your money put into stock," Mrs. Wooten said. "Your business. We'll see..."

Mr. Flagler himself congratulated Louise when she had purchased 20 shares of stock. "You're a smart girl to be so young," Mr. Flagler said when he came up from Florida during the winter of 1899 to meet with New York Governor Theodore Roosevelt and John Rockefeller. Louise and Mrs. Wooten served tea to Mr. Flagler and his guests in the library as they talked in depth about the new governor's political ambitions, the national economy, and President McKinley.

Mr. Flagler's partner was a regular visitor at the Flagler home, but Louise never got to serve him tea and cakes, which he usually took with Mr. Flagler privately in the library.

Louise read they had been partners since 1870 when the Standard Oil Company was founded. Although Rockefeller had retired from day-to-day business in 1897 and Flagler had turned his main interests to his Florida developments in hotels and a railroad in recent years, the two giants of industry counted on each other as partners still, as friends and as confidants, Louise had learned from Ida Tarbell.

Neither of the partners touched alcohol, and Mrs. Wooten was delighted when Mr. Rockefeller was a guest. "A man for all time, he is. Most of these other friends of Mr. Flagler must have their liquor. Sinful," she said.

Louise had begged to assist Mrs. Wooten when the governor and Mr. Rockefeller arrived. "Well, all right, but remember, if you spill anything or say anything, that will be the end of your appearances outside this kitchen," Mrs. Wooten warned her.

The governor did not look at Mrs. Wooten or Louise when they entered with a tea cart laden with silver service and small, fancy cakes, custard-filled chocolate éclairs, raspberry fruit tarts, and finger sandwiches of softened, sharp cheeses.

"I am not against trusts, the bigness of trusts, and obviously neither is New Jersey, allowing you to absorb your whole trust in that state under the banner of Standard of New Jersey. But regulation against monopolies—that is coming, gentlemen. That is coming," Governor Roosevelt said, pushing his rimless glasses closer to his wide nose and rubbing the end of his finger over his dark brown mustache as if he were chasing away a bug.

"You're not on the side of big business, T.R., and that is a pity. You won't serve a second term," Rockefeller said, reaching for a silver pastry server, which Louise promptly lifted and helped his plate with the pineapple tart he pointed to.

"I am not against size. I am opposed to absolute control," the governor replied.

"If you're not careful, T.R., you'll be nominated for vice president, and that will take you away from your reforms. Vice presidents are always just accessories. You've made your positions clear in New York—the taxing of corporation franchises, your conservation measures. Are you a Republican or a Democrat, T.R.?" Flagler asked.

They all laughed.

How different these men were, Louise thought. Mr. Roosevelt, round-faced, full-bodied. Mr. Rockefeller, thin, angular. Mr. Flagler was the median of the two, not too heavy or too thin. They seemed to talk and laugh for hours, drinking many cups of tea each, eating almost all the pastries and sandwiches. Louise made several trips back to the kitchen for hot water, lemon wedges, milk, and cream.

The men talked of the expected peace treaty with Spain, of Veblen's *The Theory of the Leisure Class*, which was just published, of the rising popularity of the automobile, of political unrest in the Philippines, of what might happen to monopolies, particularly in the oil industry.

When Mrs. Wooten summoned Louise to wheel the cart out, Louise was sorry she would not be able to listen in any longer. From her reading, she was able to follow the conversation of these extraordinary men. When she left the room, Louise realized that her being in the presence of such power was indeed a privilege, a special, strange kind of honor.

"Mrs. Wooten, did you hear the things they were talking about? The future of the country, the President—they all know him—war, corporations, well, things that rule the country?"

"What's it matter to you or me?" Mrs. Wooten said as she sorted the dirty dishes.

"But we heard them. We were in the same room. I felt a thrill running through me as if I had a reason for being there, listening."

"Your reason for being in the room was to serve tea and attend to Mr. Flagler and his guests. Let's get this mess cleaned up. Mr. Flagler will be going to the Rockefeller house for dinner, but there is the lot of us to eat tonight. Get busy."

There was no point in revealing her thoughts to Mrs. Wooten. The woman could not comprehend the exhilaration Louise felt at this tea or others that followed.

By the time the Spinner family of Philadelphia came to call on Mr. Flagler in the fall of 1899, Louise felt confident enough to prepare and serve tea completely on her own. She was happy when Mrs. Wooten agreed to allow Louise to wheel the cart in by herself to present the elaborate fare to his visitors.

As usual, the guests did not acknowledge the presence of a maid as Louise glanced around at the Spinners, reported to be one of the richest families in Pennsylvania. Their interests were in coal mining and oil in the East, and they were opening up exploration in the West, which Mrs. Wooten said brought them to discussions with Mr. Flagler and Mr. Rockefeller and his brother, William, an officer of the Standard. Mr. Rockefeller was entertaining them later, and they were all to gather at the William Rockefeller house for dinner.

Mr. Spinner was a portly man, finely dressed in a dark blue suit and vest. His gray-brown hair matched his wife's. Mrs. Spinner was on the plump side, too, but obviously a corset gave her body an hour-glass appearance. Her dress was a rich, green velvet, and she wore a wide-brimmed hat of the same fabric. The Spinner daughter, dressed in blue velvet, wandered about the library looking at the Chinese porcelain vases, oil landscapes, and Mr. Flagler's collection of family Bibles.

The Spinner son sat in a gold brocade chair, drinking tea. When Louise became aware that he was watching her work at the cart preparing a fresh pot of tea, she grew nervous, and, as she looked up, he winked at her. Quickly, she looked away, praying that Mrs. Wooten would come in and relieve her.

When the young man approached the cart, Louise fumbled with the pastries, dropping one against the hot tea pot so that its meringue melted, sticking to the silver.

Louise smiled nervously at the young man, who said nothing but continued to study her every move. "I can pour my own tea," he said, taking the pot, touching her hand.

"Oh, no, that is my job, sir. Let me, please."

"All right," he said, holding his tea cup higher.

Louise steadied her right hand with her left as she aimed the spout for his cup, turning the pot over gently. "There, do you take cream, milk, or lemon?"

"Nothing," he said, his brown eyes meeting hers. "Your eyes are the bluest I think I have seen," he said, staring at her intensely.

She glanced away. "Can I get you anything? A pastry?"

"No, no. Don't be nervous. I don't bite pretty girls," he said.

"Wendell, come here, Wendell. You must hear what Mr. Flagler is proposing for Key West. A railroad. How thrilling," Mrs. Spinner said.

Young Spinner winked again at Louise and turned around to face Flagler and his mother and father.

The foursome chatted about Mr. Flagler's planned project as Louise studied Wendell Spinner. He was short, just about her height, with a thin face and nose, dark brown hair plastered down with a tonic. His mischievous eyes kept darting back to her.

For once Louise was happy to see Mrs. Wooten enter the room and join her at the tea cart, but Mrs. Wooten's appearance did not dampen Wendell Spinner's interest in Louise. Leaving his parents with Mr. Flagler, he strolled back to the cart and handed his cup to Louise. "Thank you, Miss...you do have a name, don't you?"

"Miss Lambert."

"Pretty. Lyrical name pronounced in French without the 't'. Pronounced in German, no. Are you French or German? How do you pronounce your name?"

"The French way."

"You are French, then?"

"No."

"German?"

"No, no, French and Italian."

"Italian. What an extraordinary combination you are."

Louise looked at Mrs. Wooten who was fuming, her eyes flaring between the young man and Louise. Yet she did not utter a sound.

"Whatever you are, you're quite beautiful, and you can remember that Wendell Spinner said so."

"Wendell, come look at this marvelous old book," his sister called from across the room, putting her hand to her mouth when she apparently realized everyone in the large room heard her.

"Well, good-bye, Miss Lambert. I will see you again," he said.

"Don't give me any explanations. None. Maids do not flirt with guests," Mrs. Wooten warned Louise when they reached the kitchen. "I will tell Mr. Hurley, and he will take action."

"Mrs. Wooten, I did not speak to him, and I will see that he tells Mr. Hurley that on my behalf if you threaten me..."

"Well, the nerve, the gall of you, you little... I won't have this kind of talk to me...you will leave here. I can promise you that. You won't stay here with me. No respect from you. I can never have say over you, you, you horrible urchin."

Oh, why did that boy, that rich, spoiled boy have to see her, speak to her? She hated him for parading around filled with arrogance, confidence. He would not even remember talking to her, and he had probably cost her this job.

The five dozen red roses that arrived at the front entrance of the Flagler house the next day proved that Wendell Spinner did remember her, and they told Mrs. Wooten emphatically, Louise thought, that she had better not take the girl's position away. There was a possibility he would come to Louise's rescue.

"Hum," Mrs. Wooten said as she watched Louise smelling the flowers. "I suppose you'll have to use the crystal vases. We have nothing but good crystal in this house. But keep those red things out of my sight. Put them in your room."

"Sixty flowers won't fit in my room. I don't have space for that many vases, Mrs. Wooten. Take some for yourself," Louise said.

"Hum," Mrs. Wooten said, as Louise prepared vases for the other maids, Mrs. O'Donnell, Mrs. Wooten, and herself.

Louise was hypnotized by the flowers that she set in her room. Wendell Spinner, from one of the most important families in America, had sent her flowers. And they seemed, for now, to be a protective wall against Mrs. Wooten, who did not mention Louise's fate again.

Did he know she had never received flowers, had never even seen roses like this? It was a dream, wasn't it? Why had he sent them? What did he expect from her? No, she erased thoughts of sex from her mind. A maid and Wendell Spinner. No, that was ridiculous. He has dozens of beautiful girlfriends.

Somehow she must get some flowers to Cecilia. She would send them by messenger to the hospital. She could not wait to tell Carrie. On Wednesday she would see Carrie, and if the roses lasted until then, she would take some to her.

Louise had never considered the idea of using the Flagler tele-phone before, but she had to find out how Cecilia was, how she liked the flowers she had sent with a short note. No, there was no Cecilia Bellini at the hospital. She was checked out several days ago, a nun told Louise. "Keep the flowers there, will you? Give them to someone else," Louise said.

Where was Cecilia? Why didn't she write Louise a letter, make some effort to contact her? Maybe she did tell Ida Tarbell something. She could visit *McClure's* offices and ask Miss Tarbell in person.

Except for Carrie, Louise was all alone, cut off from Cecilia. Fingering the rose petals that fell on the bureau where the vase sat, Louise's visions began to chase away her reason.

She envisioned herself dancing with Wendell Spinner in an enormous ballroom. Her dress was white satin, and her hair was a mass of soft curls. She wore jewels—a diamond necklace, matching bracelets and rings, large single diamonds pinned in her hair. The ballroom flickered from the soft light of tapered candles set in ornate silver candelabra.

"French, German, Spanish, Italian, I don't care what you are, you are mine," Wendell said, as he swirled her around the room with such power and grace that she began to swoon with happiness.

Her visions were shattered with Mrs. Wooten's knocking and calling at her door.

"Open up, you silly girl. It's Mrs. O'Donnell. She's dead. The funeral is tomorrow. Be prepared," Mrs. Wooten said, not a note of sympathy or caring in her voice.

Chapter 8

On the afternoon following the death of Mrs. O'Donnell, a memorial mass was said for her at the chapel of Saint Michael's Church in mid-Manhattan. Mrs. O'Donnell's body was to be taken by rail, Mr. Hurley explained, to Titusville, Pennsylvania, and Miss Ida Tarbell was to accompany the coffin. Mrs. O'Donnell would be buried at the same grave site as her husband and son.

The organist played a sad, low tune that Louise did not recognize, but she did not feel like listening to any kind of music. Louise did not want to come to this service. She wanted to remember Mrs. O'Donnell alive, happy, bustling about in the kitchen. Why was everyone Louise loved taken away from her… or hurt severely?

Mrs. Wooten sat in the chapel's front row between Mr. Flagler and Mr. Hurley. Carrie, the other maids from the Flagler house, a few ladies from other households on Fifth Avenue, and a handful of assorted people Louise did not know filled the edifice. There was no time for the printing of a memorial announcement, the priest said, as he talked briefly about the good life of service Mrs. O'Donnell left behind as her contribution to the world. Then he spoke in Latin and knelt before a gleaming gold cross.

Mr. Flagler, Carrie said, was a Presbyterian—his father was a minister in that faith in a small town in western New York—so Louise wondered if he would get down on the kneelers like the

Catholics did. He did kneel and so did everyone else while the priest prayed for Mrs. O'Donnell's soul for the last time.

While Louise bowed her head, she felt a refreshing wave move over the whole of her being. She was not tired or sad or confused when she lifted her head and looked up at the cross. When she had entered the chapel, thoughts of tomorrow weighed her down. Where would she go? What would Mrs. Wooten do with her now, once she officially took Mrs. O'Donnell's place?

As she rose from her pew, Louise experienced a kind of peace that was new to her. She could not explain it to anyone, even to herself. She should be crying for Mrs. O'Donnell, mourning, yet she sensed that Mrs. O'Donnell would not like that. Mrs. O'Donnell was never depressed, at least outwardly.

Louise waited to speak to Ida Tarbell. The tall woman put an arm around Louise's shoulder. "Don't be afraid, Louise," she told the girl.

"I'm not, Miss Tarbell."

"Mrs. O'Donnell suffered a long time, and she is finally at rest. God bless her. And now, what about you? Will you stay at Mr. Flagler's house?"

"I don't think so, Miss Tarbell. Mrs. O'Donnell told me about jobs at Mr. Flagler's hotels in Florida, and I want to work there... in one of them."

"I could help you find another position in New York, you know."

"That's very kind of you...and I will remember that and all you've done for me."

"Well, come and see me."

"Miss Tarbell...I have wondered about Cecilia. She was hurt. Did you know?"

"I heard some awful stories about Tammany and the bosses who took over some of the houses—I didn't know about Cecilia."

"She was cut and beaten. She was in the hospital and then I lost track…"

"I can find out about Cecilia, Louise. Give me a little time. I will locate her no matter how long it takes. That's a promise," Miss Tarbell said. "Will you let me know where you go?"

"Yes, yes, I will always let you know where I am."

"God bless you," Ida Tarbell said, squeezing Louise's hands as she left her.

Carrie was waiting for Louise when she finished her visit with Miss Tarbell.

"I have a job finally," she told Louise. "Well, it isn't on the stage. But I am closer. I'm in charge of wardrobe and hairstyles. I'm even going on the road with the show. Boston. We go there first, and then to New York. Maybe even Chicago if we get the backing we need."

Glancing at Carrie as she talked, cold air forming puffs at her mouth, Louise thought Carrie was prettier than she could ever remember her. Carrie was suddenly a woman, Louise thought, full-breasted, her face filled out. She glowed when she talked about the theater. Louise wished with all her heart that she had something to enthuse her that much. There was not much in her life, she realized, except her fight to survive each day. Nothing lifted her spirits or gave her hope or dreams. Carrie took surviving for granted. She knew she would conquer tomorrow and the day after. Her bearing was secure. And so Carrie seemed near her goals. Even if they all led her to the deceptive world of make-believe.

"Are you going to Florida now that Mrs. O'Donnell has passed?" Carrie asked.

"I want to. If I can get past Mrs. Wooten. She may try to stop me. Then she may not... She's always a barrier to me."

"Oh, yes. She always will be, my dear Louise. Get away from her if you can. Right away."

"Maybe my chance will come swiftly. Mr. Flagler has called us together today. He may dismiss me," Louise said as the two girls parted.

"We are meeting here in the kitchen," Mr. Flagler told the staff after the funeral, "because I think we all feel comfortable in this room where Mrs. O'Donnell spent so much of her time. I know you all have questions about your futures, and it is my responsibility to clear the air and to lay down some roads that are open to you from here. As you know, I am spending more and more time in Florida. My wife is not getting any better, I am sad to say. This is a large house, and I am hardly ever here, and so I have decided to sell it and offer you all positions in Florida at my hotels and eventually at a house I want to build in Palm Beach."

There was complete silence as Mr. Flagler went on. "We will not be moving right away, or course, as there is much to do. We do not have a buyer for the house. There is inventory here and many details to contend with. I am asking Mr. Hurley and Mrs. Wooten to take care of this administrative work and to remain here until the house is sold. And Alex will be stationed here as my driver. Then they will go to Florida, if they choose—St. Augustine or Palm Beach. Everyone else will be going to Florida, if they choose, by the end of the year."

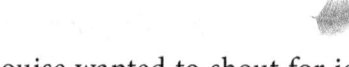

Louise wanted to shout for joy. How relieved she was. There would be no fight with Mrs. Wooten, who could not stop her now, and she apparently would not be dismissed. She was going to Florida, and maybe she would even be free of this awful woman forever. And Alex. She might never see either of them again. There was a new life waiting for her in Florida. A jungle—she wondered if Carrie knew what she was talking about.

Mrs. Wooten was not happy about leaving New York. That was all too obvious as she thrashed about the kitchen, slamming, banging pots and pans and mumbling disgustedly under her breath to everyone who asked her a question. Louise left her foe alone, hoping they would not collide.

Mr. Hurley interviewed each employee of the house during the next few days about their wishes for the future. Louise was thrilled when she said, yes, she wanted a kitchen job in the Royal Poinciana Hotel in Palm Beach.

"It's almost at the end of the United States," Mr. Hurley said. "Mr. Flagler's railroad has brought Palm Beach and Miami into the union, and he may do the same for the Florida Keys. Well, these are your instructions, then, for the trip at the end of the week. I will have train tickets for you tomorrow. Should be an exciting trip. The cars of the Mellon family of Pittsburgh, Mr. Morgan—Mr. J.P. Morgan—Mr. Whitney's car, and I believe the Wideners will be traveling along with you to Palm Beach."

"In their own private cars?"

"Yes, these families all have private cars with kitchens, drawing rooms, quarters for sleeping. You'll see the cars when you get to Florida. They go right to the door of the Poinciana Hotel, through West Palm Beach, where Mr. Flagler has many of his workers live, over Lake Worth, and then over the North Bridge to Main Street and the hotel. It is a magnificent building."

"Will I stay in West Palm Beach with the workers?"

Mr. Hurley smiled. "No, no. I did not make myself clear. The construction workers stay there in West Palm Beach. Not the maids and kitchen help. They reside in the hotel itself and in small cottages Mr. Flagler had built especially for his staff. Ah, in a way I wish I were a young, pretty girl going to Palm Beach. Anything can happen to a young lady surrounded by such... well, I am not young and I am not a girl," he smiled. "Any questions now?"

"Will I get...get to buy shares of the Standard when I..."

"Oh, yes, Mr. Flagler thought of that, too. We will, those of us in this house, continue the stock plan, but we must all keep this arrangement in confidence as Mr. Flagler does not offer this advantage to all his employees at the Poinciana. So, not a word to anyone down there."

"And what will happen after the winter season is over?"

"Do not worry about that, Miss Louise, for Mr. Flagler will need staff at the hotel through the summer, and then he did say he had plans to build a private house in Florida."

"It looks like I will never come back to New York, Mr. Hurley."

"Oh, I don't know about that. No one who has lived in New York stays away forever. What can compare to Manhattan?"

Mr. Hurley did not know her New York, did he? He has not seen how she had lived in the ghettos. Did he even know those places existed?

Before she left, she had to see Carrie and Ida Tarbell. These visits might be her last ever with the women who had, in their diverse ways, saved her life.

Carrie was washing her underclothes in the large face bowl in her room as Louise described all the preparations that were already made for her trip.

"Well, we'll both be on the road to new places, won't we? And we should be. We're young and life is ahead of us, Louise. Promise that you'll write me about your adventures in the tropics, won't you?" Carrie said, making a face like a monkey's. "Did you send that Spinner fellow a thank you for the flowers?"

"No, no...I..."

"Well, you should. I wouldn't just ignore five dozen roses."

"Where would I send a thank you note?"

"Well, let's see. They live in Philadelphia along the Main Line."

"The Main Line?"

"The Main Line of the Pennsylvania Railroad. The track runs right past the estates of the rich. They just hop on and off those big trains. They can go anywhere—to Philadelphia, New York, Chicago—right from their front doors. All the richest live along the Main Line. Well, you could address a letter to Wendell Spinner—everybody in Philadelphia knows the Spinner family. Address it to Master Spinner so the old man won't get it. You have to do that right away. You might bump into him in Palm Beach."

"They go to Palm Beach?"

"All of society goes to Palm Beach in the winter, Louise. And people who can't and think they are society say they're going there or have been."

"I don't think I will meet much of society. I'll be working in the kitchen."

"With your looks, Louise, you won't be hidden behind a stove all your life."

"I just want to earn money, you know that, Carrie, and I don't care about society. I don't know anything about society anyway."

"Well, just let me know all the names that come in and out of the hotel. It'll be good reading while I am mending men's trousers or powdering ladies' wigs or painting their faces...all the time wishing I could paint my own."

"Someday you will, Carrie. I just know that."

"I wish I did," she said.

When Louise left Carrie, she did not feel that their bond of friendship could be cut or even touched adversely by their separation. Louise knew she would see Carrie again. You do not ever break with someone who has entered your life with such force and caring and nursed you from near death back to health. Someday she might have the chance to help Carrie—though she prayed that Carrie's life and career would be marked by the best fortune anyone could imagine.

It was Cecelia who needed her now. Where was she? What was her face like now? She had to see Ida Tarbell, and so, unannounced, she walked into McClure's offices in mid-Manhattan. *McClure's Magazine*, McClure's Syndicate, Doubleday & McClure read the gold letters on the watery-looking glass door on the second floor of the tall office building. A secretary sat at a small desk in the middle of a reception room bordered all around with other glass doors, some of them open.

When Louise asked for Miss Tarbell, the young woman nodded, disappeared, returned, and led Louise to a spacious, open room filled with paper-cluttered desks, ringing telephones, and men and women working at typewriters. There was a frenzy about these offices, and Louise knew she should not have intruded. She did not belong here. She scolded herself as she was taken to Miss Tarbell's office, which opened off the large, noisy center. Her name, followed by "Editor", was printed in small gold letters on a solid, dark wood door.

"Louise," Miss Tarbell said, rising from behind her desk stacked high with leather-bound books and what she explained were manuscripts to be published in *McClure's Magazine*. "I haven't located Cecilia yet, Louise, but I have not stopped trying.

I do know that she was severely beaten, almost butchered by Margaret Dugal's bodyguards. The same night the Tammany bosses tried to take over Margaret Dugal's house. They succeeded. Margaret surrendered. Now she works for them."

"It was Margaret Dugal who had Cecilia attacked?"

"It would seem that way. Louise, I will keep trying to find her. Chances are she does not want to be found now. Margaret Dugal is vicious and would probably kill her if she found her."

"She would kill me, too, if she saw me."

"I don't think so, Louise. You are not her problem. It's the Tammany bosses who take most of her money these days. One day those houses will be shut down for good. But not soon…as long as the political leaders of New York are actually operating the houses. It is a pity you had to be part of that world, Louise. I hope your future won't take you near that way of life again. I… Mr. McClure, Mr. Baker…" Ida Tarbell said. Two short men who looked as if they could be brothers burst into her office.

The older man, with tousled, sandy-colored hair and a bushy mustache to match, waved his hands over his head. "That damn Frank Doubleday. I wish I had never heard of him or J.P. Morgan or made the bond agreement for my company and taken over Harper & Brothers. Doubleday should stick to his book publishing and not meddle in every venture of mine. They tell… they tell me, Ida, that *McClure's* alone will gross over $400,000 in ads this year. We are the most successful magazine in the country—beating *Munsey's, Ladies' Home Journal, The Atlantic, Harper's, The Cosmopolitan*, all of them—and that this will be our best year. We have the highest circulation in the land—and we'll come out in the red? Damn it!" he shouted.

"Mr. McClure," the younger man said. Like McClure, he had a less bushy mustache, brownish hair, a rounder, pudgier face,

and slower, more contemplative eyes. "Mr. McClure, Booth Tarkington is here…and Charles Dana Gibson about the illustrations
for Mr. Tarkington's article…"

"I don't give a damn. Ray, let me talk to Ida. She'd the
damn editor of this magazine. Well, I don't understand it, Ida,
with all the money. I don't understand it. I should never have
made the damn deal with J.P. Morgan. I am not a financier. He
fleeces everybody. Ray, go tell them to wait. Kipling's coming in
here, too, in a minute. We'll go to lunch at the Waldorf. No, the
Holland House." McClure glanced at Louise. "Sorry, little girl, I
had to come in here like this."

"Mr. McClure…" Ida said.

"Yes, yes, I know you need time off. We'll talk about it this
afternoon. You look pale. You could use a rest cure but not in
Titusville with your family. Some place quiet. We'll talk about it."

The men were suddenly gone, and Louise felt as if a strong
wind had just swept past her.

"I didn't know you weren't feeling good…"

"I am fine, Louise. Tired. Mr. McClure has been away in
Europe. There has been a lot on my shoulders. I will find Cecilia
or put her in touch with you. Don't worry. I won't disappear."

"I'll be working at the Royal Poinciana Hotel."

"I'm glad about that, Louise. So I will write you there. Stay
well, Louise, and if you need me, you will seek me out. I don't
plan to leave New York ever. I will be right here close to Mr.
McClure until the day he dies…more than likely."

What a stable, sure woman Ida Tarbell was, Louise thought
as she made her way back to the Flagler mansion. If only I could
find that security in my life. She knows where she is going and
how to get there. If I could find out where I was going…I am
always running…but where?

When she was back in her room, her bags packed, the list of instructions before her with the rail tickets for her journey south, Louise wrote out a short note to Wendell Spinner and sealed and stamped it. *He will probably never get this. I will not see him again, anyway. The flowers were a whim. A rich gentleman's way of toying with a maid.*

Thoughts of Wendell Spinner lingered with her when she left the Flagler house in a carriage bound for Pennsylvania Station and as she boarded the New York Central Railroad car that would connect in Jacksonville with Mr. Flagler's Florida East Coast Railroad. Several passengers around her talked about the fancy private cars at the end of the train. The car that would take her to Palm Beach was beautiful to her, with its dark green mohair seats topped with white linen headrest covers.

Negro men, dressed in starched white shirts, walked up and down the aisle passing out puffy bed pillows covered with white slips smelling as if they had just come from the laundry. A conductor in a black cap and suit with gold buttons collected blue tickets from passengers. When Louise handed the man her tickets, he grinned at her and punched some of the small papers. "All the way to Florida. Well, now, you're about 30 hours away from that great state of sunshine. Enjoy your trip, little lady," he said.

The train finally moved from the platform, through a dark, cavernous network of steel and concrete, and into the sunlight, past tall buildings, through familiar tenement sections and factories belching black smoke, and finally to strings of small wood houses and the countryside.

As the train moved south, the conductor announced each state. When they were crossing the Pennsylvania border into

Maryland, it started to snow, sheets of white blocking out the scenery as twilight descended. The next morning when the train rolled into North Carolina, the snow-covered ground was replaced by a gray-brown landscape of leafless trees. Just before they pulled into the Savannah terminal, Louise spotted patches of green grass. The next morning they would be in Florida, the conductor promised, in "the land of sun and oranges."

Louise felt she had been on the train forever when they did reach Florida, yet it was not until the engine and track switchover in Jacksonville that she realized the trip was ending. She had arrived in her new home. It did not look like a jungle. It was more a kind of colorful wilderness dotted with tall, skinny pine and moss-draped oak trees that grew along wide, black-water canals topped with purple lilies.

Carrie was wrong. This country was not inhabited by anyone, animal or man. Only plants and trees. So thick was the vegetation in some sections that Louise could not imagine men fighting their way through to build a railroad. It was the sunlight, the brilliant, clear sunlight that captivated the girl. This must be like the Sicily my mother loved. And the water, where is the ocean, where are the lakes that are supposed to be everywhere in Florida? At almost the time Louise asked the question, the lake country appeared.

The center of the state was a lace-work of water ways. By the time they reached Fort Pierce and Stuart, the foliage began to change. Flowers—red, pink, violet, gold—endless vines climbing even over the bright yellow wooden depots bearing the name of Florida East Coast, fan-leaved palmettos, orange and grapefruit trees, and so many more plants she had not read about formed a picture of lushness she would never forget.

After a stop in West Palm Beach, the train rumbled and clattered over tracks running over a wooden bridge spanning Lake Worth. Slowly, the engineer braked the train, and when it was stopped finally, Louise saw an enormous bright yellow wood building, the same color as the depots in the towns the train had passed throughout state.

A young boy wearing a wide-billed cap, a blue vest, and dark pants jumped aboard Louise's car and called her name.

"Here I am," she said automatically, the sound of her voice startling her after its long silence.

"Come with me," he said, "I'll take you to the kitchen manager of the hotel."

With her small valise which contained everything she owned—all once belonging to Carrie—Louise walked quickly, almost running to keep up with the boy.

Through a lobby—with tall, potted palms, green carpeting, white wicker furniture, standing groups of ladies in long white dresses and men in white suits with straw top hats—the young pair glided.

The boy led her through a series of hallways until they reached the kitchen, which to Louise seemed more like a huge barn in size. It was brimming with stainless steel pots—four times the size of Mr. Flagler's largest copper pans—metal stirring utensils, men in tall white chef hats and women in gray uniforms, the kind Louise herself had worn at the Flagler house.

A heavy-set woman with a light blue dress came forward from a desk at the back of the kitchen.

"Mrs. Glenn," she said, offering the girl her hand. "Mr. Hurley says you are a fine kitchen girl and we need one. Alfred will get you to your place, and when you unpack, come back here. There's lots to do."

Chapter 9

Louise was told there were at least three miles of hallways in the Royal Poinciana Hotel, and for the first week of her work there—in the sprawling building that faced Lake Worth—she decided she had walked every step of the expanse. Since one of the breakfast order girls was taken sick with a cold, Louise was sent around at 11 at night to pick up breakfast cards which guests hung on their outside doorknobs if they wanted breakfast in their rooms.

Almost 1,200 guests were registered now in the 800 rooms which sat in six stories on acres filled with big red, pink, and yellow flowers and swaying palm trees. Guests were paying about 100 dollars a day to stay at this hotel, and Louise longed to see more of the wood structure than the hallways and the kitchen, but her tour would have to wait. Now she had the opportunity not only to work in the kitchen cleaning and cutting celery, green pole beans, lettuce, and tomatoes—brought in daily from Belle Glade which lay west of West Palm Beach—but she could pick up extra money serving relish dishes to tables in the dining room which seated 1,600.

When Louise finished her days, which ran from six in the morning until midnight, she fell into her narrow bed in the small room painted light green, as all the halls and rooms in the hotel seemed to be. There was no time to do anything but bathe in the shower room down the hall, sleep, and try to recover energy for the next day. In a way she was happy. Mrs. Glenn was strictly a businesswoman, and she ran the kitchen staff with great precision, logging the staff members' times in and out, days off—Louise chose none—and passing out payroll checks each week.

Louise could not believe the enormous army it took to operate the hotel—you could get lost in the crowd of them, about 1,700 employees. There was a waiter for every four diners, a chamber maid for every two rooms, a bellman in every hall. More than 100 people were spread through the kitchen from breakfast till after dinner. There were bread bakers, pastry chefs, meat grillers, vegetable cooks, salad girls—like Louise—and many other specialists.

Louise was amazed at the huge sides of beef and lamb delivered to the coolers, the number of vegetable and egg crates stacked high at the back doors every morning, the tubs of shrimp and fish brought from the boats by the local fishermen, the fresh-picked citrus fruits from Mr. Flagler's groves, the whipping cream, butter and milk delivered by truck from farms in the Glades. The array of foods—from the ornate, chocolate and vanilla cakes to the intricate jellied molds in the shapes of fish and lobster—overwhelmed Louise. Not even in Mr. Flagler's house had she seen such magic performed for meals.

There was a pageantry about the parade of food moving into the hotel each day—the bright colors, the freshness, the smells of it all made Louise hungry before she was able to stop for a cup of coffee and a fresh-baked sweet roll every morning.

She wanted to learn every recipe, and she could, Mrs. Glenn promised, when the season slowed down in February, toward the end of the season. The cooks would be able to show her some of their tricks. When the assistant to the poissonnier left abruptly,

Mrs. Glenn asked Louise to fill in, and Louise gladly accepted the additional job.

Every morning, Jonas Redmond, one of the men who fished for the hotel, brought in the largest catches from Lake Worth and from the Atlantic Ocean which was only several hundred yards east of the hotel. Iced down in his metal chests were red snapper, pompano, and bluefish. He carried the containers in his bronzed, muscular arms to the walk-in ice boxes. The fish entrées were prepared to order from the harvests Jonas and other suppliers had brought in only hours before.

After more than two weeks of logging in the daily fish bounties, Louise finally began to talk to Jonas about his treasures from the sea and inland waterway, Lake Worth.

"The waters are always brimming," Jonas said, his blue-green eyes lighting up when the girl showed an interest in his boat and special fishing techniques.

"I'll take you out on the boat one day, Louise, when you get time off."

"That's hardly ever," she said. "I work every day."

"Maybe on Sunday."

"Sunday, too. I work on Sunday."

"Well, when you get some time. Some day you'll slow down, and I can show you what's around this hotel. I'll bet you don't know you're living in the middle of a jungle."

"Yes, yes, I know," Louise said, remembering Carrie's warnings.

"This is a beautiful part of the world. I'll be your guide, if you like."

"Yes, I would like that, Mr. Redmond." Stopping her routine counting the fish delivered, Louise looked at Jonas Redmond for a minute. His wide face was glazed a golden brown and so were his arms and legs, which she could see from his ankles up to his knees since he had rolled up his pants still wet from fishing. Jonas' straight brown hair was thick and sun-streaked blond. His shoulders were broad, his hands thick, strong, sure. How old was he—25 or more. He regarded her, she thought, as a child. He has no idea what lies behind me, that I am old for my years. I could handle anything he might pull. After all, he is a man.

"All right," she said, "one of these days I'll say yes and we'll go around the island."

When he smiled, she saw straight white teeth. How healthy he was. Yes, he appeared exactly as she would expect a man of Florida, a fisherman who lived in the sun and water, to look. But more, there was a fineness about him that she liked immediately—she had seen it in no other man she had met. Still, how many men had she known? Alex, Wendell Spinner, Mr. Flagler, boys in her classes back in New York. I don't know any men well, Louise thought. And I can't judge this man yet. I can take him or leave him, she sighed, reminding herself that men usually were after females' bodies and nothing more.

When Mrs. Glenn insisted that Louise rest on the upcoming Thursday, Louise told Jonas that she was finally ready to accept his offer.

"Where did you come from, Louise?" Jonas asked as they walked by foot to the wide golden beaches meeting the Atlantic.

"From back in New York. And you. Where are you from?"

"South Carolina, Charleston," he said. "When I was just a boy my pappy brought me here. He became a fisherman, a mailman, the general storekeeper. I followed in his footsteps."

"And where is he now?"

"Died a few years ago. The store was washed away by a hurricane, and I took the job as the mailman to Miami."

"You're not a mailman anymore?"

"No, Mr. Flagler's railroad came through in 1896 and the train delivers mail to Miami now."

"How did you get there, to Miami," she said.

"I walked."

"You walked. How far is it?"

"A long, long walk. Takes a couple of days on foot."

"How did you get through the jungle?"

"You walk on the beaches. That's the only open space... or was," he said, as they watched the waves break, roll in as gushing foam, hug and pull the shoreline, and return to the sea tamed, dissolved.

"Well, I've got a good job now. Keeps me busy catching enough fish for all those rich folks to enjoy in your hotel," Jonas said.

"That's all you do?"

"In the winter. In the summer I build, paint houses, do odd jobs for the hotels, people over in West Palm, fish some, too."

"Where do you live?"

When they had walked about a mile, she guessed, they came to a hut set back from the lake about 50 feet. It was surrounded by lacy ferns; red and pink hibiscus; coconut palms, their tops bearing clusters of round, green-brown fruit; trees whose branches drooped with oranges, grapefruits, and lemons, all as big as one of Jonas' hands. The shack was woven of palmetto fronds.

"That's it," he said, "this is home. Come on in."

Jonas' front door was wide enough for them to enter abreast. Made of smaller fronds than the roof, the door was framed in driftwood and attached to the walls by metal hinges that squeaked when Jonas closed it.

The house was one big room. A battered, round wood table stood in the center. It held an apple-green glass bottle with three wide-lipped yellow flowers.

"Alamandas," Jonas said. "The flowers are Alamandas." When he opened double doors at the rear of the house, Louise could not believe the range of colors behind them. Sprays of pink and purple and white orchids popped from cabbage palms; massive blooming vines of salmon, coral, and fuchsia bougain-villea looked like paper blooms. A huge, umbrella-shaped tree bearing clusters of tiny orange flowers shaped like spoons stood blushing as a backdrop.

"The royal poinciana," Jonas lifted a hand toward the canopy of the tree. "They even named the hotel after that tree. I call it the flame tree. It usually blooms twice a year, now and again in late May and through June. But sometimes it surprises me. Independent tree."

Louise thought she must surely have stepped into paradise. Heaven could not be more beautiful, greener, more exquisitely painted.

"You must be very happy here," Louise said, as Jonas squeezed orange juice and broke open a coconut, punching one of the rings in its face with his penknife.

Then he poured the coconut's clear white milk into the orange juice.

"Here," he said, handing her the glass.

"It's wonderful, Jonas."

"I'll give you a dinner you'll never forget, too. Fried fish, scal-lions, green peppers, corn on the cob, and maybe I'll throw in a sweet potato and some pineapple."

"Where are you going to get all that food?"

"I caught the fish earlier...and my garden. It's down past

the flame tree. I grow the best scallions anywhere, the biggest peppers, too."

"All right here? Who owns this land, Jonas?"

"I do. I'm a squatter and by legal rights, it's mine. Mr. Flagler must have gotten into your head with a question like that. Ownership. The good Lord owns it all. We're just borrowing. Nobody owns any of this. Not even Mr. Flagler, and from what I know of him, he'd be the first to admit that. Deeds, squatters' rights. They're all man's inventions. Well, I'm borrowing hundreds of acres along the beaches and the lake, down as far as Miami."

"What do you mean by that?"

"Well, my daddy got deeded land when he ran the store. People would give him an acre here and another there for supplies or payment on their accounts. I have all those deeds and others I've picked up on my own."

"You must be rich."

He laughed.

"No, Louise. I'm not rich. This is old swamp land and, except for Mr. Flagler's railroad through here and the hotels, there's not a lot going on. Most people think Florida is a waste. And in many parts, it still is."

"I didn't mean rich in money," she said, "but in land and the way you live. You have everything you want to eat, and you're never cold—not in this sunshine—and you have water everywhere to swim in and fish from. Yes, you are rich."

Louise was suddenly aware she had made a discovery. There was a different way of life other than the extremes that trapped people in New York. Jonas has the best of everything here. He is rich, richer than he might ever realize. Or did he know? He had lived somewhere else, in South Carolina, where it was cold and people were poor. She had read about its reconstruction after the war, its Negroes, and white carpetbaggers. No, South Carolina was not like this.

Jonas was an encyclopedia on Florida, and he told Louise about its discovery by the Spanish and its development through the years. "Mr. Flagler has the greatest vision of anyone who has ever come to these shores," he said, "even though he did put me out of work on my mail route. I guess I can forgive him for that small trespass. He has a lot bigger things in store for this state, and we'll all be better off because of him."

"How could you be better off?"

"As fine as this life is, Louise, we need real settling. We need hospitals and doctors and education for our children. We are a wilderness still, not that far away from the Indian days. Man's got to progress. I don't want this land torn apart to put up hotels, but we'll have to sacrifice something for the civilizing that's got to come. I saw my own daddy die for want of a doctor…and there have been lots of others, my friends, who died and suffered because we had no doctor or hospital."

Even paradise has its weaknesses, Louise thought as she listened to Jonas.

As the day turned into an afternoon of golden sunlight and then into a blue-violet twilight, Louise realized she could listen to Jonas talk forever. After he cooked the meal he promised on an open fire behind the hut, they lay down outside on a soft bed of brown Australian pine needles he had gathered from under the trees surrounding the hotel. The moon was just beginning to show through the deep purple shadows of the sky. When it was dark, he turned to her. "How about a swim?"

"I don't have a bathing suit," she said.

"You don't need a suit. You can just go in…"

"Naked?"

"No one will see you. Maybe God. That's all."

He was like all the rest, wasn't he? "Never," she said, jumping up. "I have to get back to the hotel."

Jonas sat up. "I won't touch you. I won't do anything to you that you don't want me to. I won't look at you in the water. I just meant the water feels good and you should try it. I don't want anything else from you."

"I still have to go. I have to get up early."

"All right," he said, and they walked in silence along a moon-lighted path back to the hotel.

Chapter 10

Louise felt cut off from the world as she lost herself in her work at the hotel. Her only recreation was reading the books which Ida Tarbell had given her and which Mr. Hurley had shipped to her in Palm Beach.

For Louise, New York did not exist. There was no word from Ida Tarbell about Cecilia. Carrie sent her a postcard from a small town in Connecticut where her last show had closed. The remainder of the hotel was not here for Louise, either, for it was filled with the richest people in America and the titled of Europe, and she could not appear in the lobby in her uniform or the modest dresses she owned.

Very late at night and before dawn, she did steal into the lobby and rotunda, the ballroom, the drawing rooms, the tea garden—Coconut Grove—to see where guests spent their time. If no one was around, she would rock herself into a drowsiness in one of the high-backed, white wicker chairs that sat on the wide veranda fronting the building.

Louise saw Jonas on her days off, infrequent as they were, and he always offered her a safe swim. Finally, one night after a sumptuous dinner of baked bananas, pompano—which he had caught that afternoon in the ocean—fried potatoes and crisp, dark green lettuce, she was ready to try to swim. She undressed behind the hut, hanging her clothes over an orange tree branch and wrapping herself in a towel until she reached the lake. She tested it with a toe. It was cool and, as she looked out over the expanse, she was hypnotized by the shimmering flecks of moon-light dancing endlessly before her.

Jonas was already swimming. She could not admit to him she could not swim. She had only waded and dunked herself in the East River when she went out on a raft with some of her class-mates. There was never time to learn to swim. She squatted down in the water, which covered her body, and watched Jonas sailing, his strokes moving him quickly.

"Come on," he called to her.

"Later," she said. "This feels so good right here."

Louise tried to paddle, her hands and her feet still touching the fine, sandy bottom of Lake Worth.

Jonas swam to her and took her hands, pulling her to him.

"I can't swim," she said.

"I'll teach you. It's easy. Comes naturally. Here, cup your hands like this. Relax, work with the water, don't fight it."

After practicing what Jonas was teaching her, she was able to propel her body a few feet and then she sank, frightened by her closeness to Jonas. Here they were in the water, bare, drenched in silver light. He wouldn't do anything she did not want him to. The words rolled over and over in her mind as she splashed water toward him, laughing.

Her body was filled with sensations she had not felt before. She wanted Jonas to hold her. Yet she knew what would happen if he did.

"I have to go…" she said, as he took her in his arms and kissed her.

Their bodies were weightless in the water, suspended in time, and Louise felt they were riding on a cloud as Jonas lifted her body and turned her around in front of him so that her back was touching his chest. He swam with her behind him, one of his arms under her breasts. She touched his arm—the strength, the muscles of it filled her with security. As Jonas pulled her along with him, waves peeled away from either side of her body.

When they went ashore, his arms around her, she was chilled. He covered her with a towel, and they sat by the fire, drinking coffee that he brewed in a heavily chipped, gray enamel pot.

"You're a beautiful woman," he said, touching her long black hair that fell in curls around her shoulders.

His eyes glistened in the firelight, and his tanned skin shone. She wanted to hold Jonas. They both knew it. One day we will, she told herself. Why is nature so cruel? Why does it punish you, threaten you when you want love and need it? A baby. I can't get pregnant again. I would want a child with Jonas, but would he want a baby? He's never said he loves me or talked of marriage… or children.

Retreating from the fire and gathering her clothes, Louise looked at Jonas. He was everything there was to want in a man, a husband. His shack was a home, not the kind she dreamed of in New York, but a home. She could live with Jonas in that shack and raise children and be happy for the rest of her life. She wondered if he had any idea of the extent of her thoughts.

The winter in Palm Beach was turning into spring before February—with hardly any weather change that Louise could see. But Jonas pointed out the subtle color differences winter's passing brought to the island. The leaves grew into a deeper green, the sweet fragrance of white jasmine diffused perfume everywhere, the sunny days were longer, the sunsets a more brilliant red.

As the winter season ended with the Flagler's annual Washington's birthday party, the crowds of visitors at the hotel boarded Mr. Flagler's trains or their private cars and traveled back to their homes in the East and Midwest.

Only a skeleton crew remained at the hotel, and Louise found herself doing various odd jobs that Mrs. Glenn assigned her— flushing the toilets in the hotel at least once a week to keep rust stains from forming in the bowls, pulling up shades and opening windows to let fresh air circulate, turning mattresses, taking inventories of the kitchen equipment and canned foods.

Through November and the re-election of President McKinley and the election of Theodore Roosevelt as vice president, there was such a quiet on the island that Louise thought Palm Beach had been severed from the mainland. Jonas was happy when everyone was away, he said, because he was able to stop fishing, tend his gardens, travel by foot along the Atlantic coast, and think.

When Louise thought, she drifted back to New York, to Cecilia, to Ida Tarbell, to Wendell Spinner, to Carrie, even to Mrs. Wooten and Alex who, she learned in early December, were coming to work at the hotel in Palm Beach.

The Flagler house was sold the month before, and Mr. Flagler was now a citizen of Florida. Around the hotel, the rumor was that Mr. Flagler had been seeing a woman for years and wanted to marry her and would ask Florida to pass an act stating that incurable insanity was a ground for divorce. New York had no such law.

Louise could not blame Mr. Flagler for searching for his freedom wherever he could find it. He had apparently kept his romance a secret from his staff—or had they just not talked about it?

When the new season began, the hotel staff buzzed with news of Mr. Flagler's impending divorce and his long courtship of Miss Mary Lily Kenan, from a fine North Carolina family.

When Mrs. Wooten and Alex arrived at the Poinciana, Mrs. Glenn insisted that Louise greet them at the train since she did not know Mrs. Wooten or the driver from New York.

"Hum," Mrs. Wooten said when she saw Louise standing by the steps of her car, "you've gone native. Brown and fat."

Alex simply nodded at Louise, and they both followed the girl to their quarters on the same floor as Louise's. "I will be in charge here of all china, silver, serving pieces, the complete inventory," Mrs. Wooten said.

"What will you do, Alex?" Louise asked.

"Well, drive, of course. Mr. Flagler is having a new Oldsmobile shipped down. Well, several, in fact. I will drive his exclusively."

"I suppose our paths won't cross much at the hotel, Miss Louise. But when Mr. Flagler builds his house, we might all be together again," Mrs. Wooten said as Louise left her at her room.

She wished with all her heart that she would never again report to Mrs. Wooten. Her mere presence, even in this large building, made Louise shudder.

As the hotel swelled with famous, rich guests, Louise fell into her regular work routine, seeing Jonas on her days off. She prayed that Mr. Flagler would not request her to join his household staff if Mrs. Wooten was going to be among the managers. And Alex. Couldn't Louise remain on the staff here? Well, she would worry about that later. Now the season was on, her savings and her stock in Standard Oil were growing, and she felt some peace at the hotel, in her room, and with Jonas.

"You know, Jonas, I live for these days with you," she told him.

"Then why not make every day our day?" he said. "Let's get married."

"Yes," she said. "I can still earn money. I can still work at the hotel…"

"No, no wife of mine works for anyone. We can live here, Louise. I can provide for us. I don't want you working anywhere."

"I…but I'm saving money and I am buying…"

"Why is it important to you to work at the hotel?"

"Jonas, I've been poor…so long."

"Trust me, Louise, you won't be poor with me. You don't need that job at the hotel or any job. Come and be my wife, and I will give you a life that will make you happy. We'll have babies…"

Pitted against the reality of what Jonas was saying, images of Mr. Flagler's great house, of Wendell Spinner sweeping through her head, Louise held her face in her hands. Did she really want to live in this shack and have children here? What about the doctors Jonas talked about and a better life? She wanted something more than this. Jonas was rich in everything but real money. He could not provide a stone house, electric lights, nice clothes. And Cecilia. How could she ever help Cecilia if she married Jonas?

Louise did not see Jonas for the next several weeks. She could not bear to tell him no, that she could not marry him. Yes, she loved him. She knew she always would…but marriage. Now? No. Why did she have to think about Wendell Spinner? He was simply a memory. No, less…an imaginary character, someone she would never see again.

When a letter arrived from Ida Tarbell, Louise's heart leaped. She had been ill and away from New York for a long time, yet her search for Cecilia went on, she explained to Louise. There seemed to be no trace of her. Even the hospital where Cecilia was treated had no address for her. All her bills were paid when she left. Margaret Dugal still operated her house on Fourteenth Street, and the politicians' control of houses of prostitution was more rampant than ever, Miss Tarbell said.

Lost in her dilemma over Jonas, Louise went about her jobs at the hotel mechanically until one evening when she was serving relishes to her assigned tables in the dining room. Usually she did not look carefully at the guests, but when she approached one of her tables for four, she recognized the young woman as Wendell Spinner's sister and the older people, yes, they were the Spinners, his parents. Of course, they did not respond to Louise. Why would they remember one of Mr. Flagler's maids?

"Louise," said a voice beside her. "What luck. I thought it was you. Louise Lambert. French, Italian, Spanish. Whatever."

Wendell Spinner pulled out his chair, smiling at Louise. "What absolute good fortune. I knew you were here, I should confess. I found out before we came. Well, cheers," he lifted a glass of water to his parents. His mother frowned.

"Wendell," Mrs. Spinner said. "Really, Wendell." His mother glanced Louise's way, avoiding her eyes.

Bracing herself against the serving station which held flatware and extra relish dishes, Louise counted the minutes until she could make an exit. She could not disappear until after the soup course. She was afraid of Wendell. What would she say to him? Thank him again for the roses? Would he remember that he sent them to her? His mother was annoyed, she was sure, that he had spoken to a waitress, even worse, perhaps, to a former maid.

Louise watched Wendell as he ate. He was better looking than she remembered him. He wore a white suit which complimented his skin, reddish-pink from swimming or tennis, she assumed.

He knew she was here. Had he come to see her? How foolish of me to think this way, she kept telling herself. His family are friends of Mr. Flagler, and they are all in high society. Wendell's being here has nothing to do with me.

Using all her will power, Louise stood motionless in the dining room watching her tables. She would make another round to see if anyone wanted more celery, olives, pickles, or herring in cream, and then she would run away. If only she did not have to go to Wendell's table again. As she approached the Spinners, Mrs. Spinner held up her hand and shook her head, indicating there was no need to serve them again. No one else at the table seemed to notice Mrs. Spinner's command.

In the kitchen, Louise felt total relief. Surely Wendell would not come back here. Why didn't he just ignore her? Why did she feel this way? Her stomach churned. She could not remember being this flighty or nervous. Butterflies in her tummy—that's what people said when they felt this way.

She could run to Jonas and never see Wendell again. That would be that. You know there can never be anything between you and Wendell Spinner, now don't you, Louise lectured herself.

Wendell Spinner is an extremely rich man. You are a very poor kitchen girl. Why are you dreaming—and what are you dreaming? How dare you waste your time. Put your hours to good use. Work, earn money, and stop being foolish. Anyway, do you care about him? I must, she thought, or why did I get so nervous when I saw him? Am I convincing myself that I like him because I know he has everything that would take me away from being doomed to poverty? Is that why my stomach is upset? Because of his money?

At this moment, Wendell was probably strolling among the

acres of tropical flowers and palms with a ravishing young lady as rich as he was. He might be kissing her now in the moonlight.

"Oh, Jonas, why can't you have money? You have everything else," she said to herself.

Chapter 11

Six dozen roses—twelve each of pink, yellow, white, peach, red, and violet—were waiting in clear glass vases for Louise when she checked into the kitchen in the morning. Mrs. Glenn smiled and patted Louise on the back. "I don't know who he is, but he's after you, my girl," she said.

The kitchen staff sniffed the flowers, and a few of the girls giggled and said they wished they had rich beaus like Louise's.

"Mrs. Glenn," Louise said, glancing at the assorted flowers, "please take one of these for yourself and give the others to ladies who would enjoy them."

"I will, indeed. You're a very generous girl, Louise. Thank you."

Louise carried the yellow roses back to her room and on the way read the small card:

> *Roses are red and purple and greenish-blue, and no one could ever be so pretty as you.*
>
> *W. Spinner*
>
> *P.S. Have a picnic with me tomorrow. I know you have the day off.*

"I can't believe this," she said aloud.

At noon, Wendell was at the same table he had shared with

his parents the night before. He was alone. Louise had to talk to him. With a relish dish in her hand, she approached him.

"Mr. Spinner...please don't get up. I...I appreciate the flowers. They...they are magnificent. But I can't..."

"You can't? Why not? Am I not perfectly acceptable to you? I'll meet you in the lobby tomorrow at 11. I have hired an Afro-mobile, ordered lunch from here, and all I need is you. It's all settled," he said, opening his foot-long menu.

"Mr. Spinner, I don't think you understand...I work here. I..."

"Yes, yes, I know. I am well aware of that. I never take no for an answer. Like your illustrious boss, Mr. Flagler. It's settled."

There was no use arguing with him, and Louise felt awkward even talking with a guest at such length. She would meet him and tell him no, that she could not go and that she could not accept his attentions. She would be dismissed at once for meeting with a hotel guest.

To appear in the hotel's common amenity rooms, Louise had to dress in her very best, which was one of Carrie's old summer dresses. It was a purple frock faded now to a pale violet, but Louise had no choice but to wear it to decline Wendell's invitation and to try to explain her situation as an employee of the hotel.

When she arrived in the lobby, she could not find Wendell. She sat down in a green velvet chair and watched the parade of guests. They were all perfectly dressed and groomed. Mechanized mannequins; did they have any feelings beneath those manicured exteriors? As they moved about greeting one another, smiling, laughing, they appeared to be completely carefree, unaware that a world beyond them existed. If only they could imagine all of the preparations being made at this minute for their lunch, their tea, their dinner. And the human sweat pouring out for their comfort and visual pleasure. The cooks, the maids, the gardeners, the managers pooled their efforts to create this wonderland from behind a wall of invisibility.

The guests did not wonder how these fantasies were produced—they just expected the best of everything life, and Flagler, had to offer, and they received what they paid for.

Would any one of them believe that right now a young man was out battling the sea to catch their lunch and dinner? Jonas, dear, sweet, gentle Jonas. She wished he were here to help her.

After waiting 15 minutes, Louise was beginning to think Wendell was not serious about a picnic anyway. What a relief. Then, he suddenly appeared, bowed from the waist when he saw her, and put his arm out for hers.

"You don't understand," she said. "I can't accept your invitation. I didn't come here to go anywhere."

"Yes, it is a lovely day, isn't it? I am so glad you decided to come," he said, as though he could not hear her. "I am hard of hearing. Whatever it is you're saying, you'll have to shout."

Exasperated, Louise stopped, shaking her head. He couldn't hear her! She pulled his arm back and tapped his cheek. "Look at me. Can you read lips?"

"No, I don't know what you're saying. Come along, our Afro-mobile is waiting."

Past the veranda, on the path leading to the ocean, waited an open white wicker carriage attended by a white-bearded Negro. He took off his hat to greet the couple. Wendell helped Louise into the wicker, two-passenger carriage that was to be pedaled along on three bicycle wheels by the Negro whose single perch was just behind their seat.

"He's taking us to a picnic spot near the ocean under some

trees, and then he'll come back for us after lunch," Wendell said, his eyes set straight ahead.

There was no use talking if he could not hear. So Louise enjoyed the short ride to the beach to a clearing on the gold sand set with small black wrought iron tables and chairs. Wendell picked out a table made private by a hedge of sea grape shrubs and opened the natural-colored straw picnic basket he had ordered from the hotel kitchen, he noted. Lined with a red-checkered cloth, the basket contained a bowl of potato salad decorated with pimento-stuffed olives, a platter of crisp fried chicken, an ice-filled bucket with white wine, and a loaf of warm French bread.

As he unpacked the food and set the marble-top table, Louise sat down as if she were not part of his picnic but an observer. Her disinterest did not seem to deflate Wendell's enthusiasm at all.

"I am not giving up on you," he said.

"What?" she said, almost whispering.

"I said I am not…"

"You can hear. That was a terrible trick," she said. "Why, why did you do it?"

"Because I had to have you come with me."

He poured the wine into two hollow-stemmed glasses. "Here's to us, my dear Louise.

"I don't drink wine."

"Ah, a Flagler girl through and through. Not even a taste?"

"No," she said.

"You and my mother are quite alike. You'll find out someday."

"I have to get back," she said, growing more fearful every minute that someone she knew from the hotel would see her with young Spinner and report her. There was simply no fraternization allowed between guests and hotel staff. Mrs. Glenn had made that clear often enough. If Mrs. Wooten got a glimpse of this meeting, Louise would not work another minute at the hotel.

"Let me speak frankly," Wendell said as they ate their lunch, Louise picking at hers. "I think you are ravishing, and I aim to have you."

"Mr. Spinner. I am a kitchen…"

"I know what you do. I don't care about that," he said, his eyes dark and intense as he studied her face. "I care about what you are going to do and be. All right. Do you understand?"

"No, I…don't, Mr. Spinner."

"It's Wendell, Louise. My name is Wendell. I don't think you realize what I am saying to you."

"No, I don't at all."

"We'll have a proper courtship…about a week…and then we'll get married."

"Are you mad?" she asked, her head shaking in disbelief, her hands beginning to tremble. "You don't know me, Mr. Spinner."

"I know you're beautiful and young, and you're not one of those dull débutantes I've had thrown at me. But that's all beside the point."

"You're proposing that I marry you? Your family…"

"Hang the family. It's my life," he said, jumping up to refill his wine glass. "Drink your wine. Let's at least have a toast," he said, holding his glass up to hers. Louise gulped the wine and at once it made her hot inside and then dizzy. This was some kind of prank Wendell had concocted. Proposing to her. She rose and started to walk away from him.

"I'm not joking, you know, Louise. I am going to have you one way or another."

Did wine make you so lightheaded that you could not walk? No, it was the sun and Wendell's absurd ideas.

Later in the afternoon, remembering the incident at lunch from which she had walked away in a stupor, Louise tried to make some sense of Wendell's actions. Then she was sure she had dreamed of Wendell's proposal. None of it really happened.

When she did not see him or hear from him for days, she was certain the sun and tropics were getting to her.

She had real things to think about now. Mr. Flagler obtained his divorce, after several years trying, on August 12, 1901, and he married Miss Mary Lily Kenan on August 24th.

Mr. Flagler had earlier planned a fairy-tale mansion and bought the land for it in 1893, Louise was told. He completed the great house, which sat at the edge of Lake Worth, in the winter of 1902 and the couple moved in February 6th.

This wonder of a home was presented to the bride, whose age was 34, as a wedding gift by her groom, whose years numbered 71 at the time of the union.

The self-made tycoon called his production Whitehall, and the *New York Herald* described it as "...more wonderful than any palace in Europe, grander and more magnificent than any other private dwelling in the world." Louise read the article about the unbelievable present over and over, hardly believing its size and grandeur.

The island was suddenly thrown into a state of chaos as the great house blossomed into a home. Louise, Mrs. Wooten, and Alex were all invited to join the staff by Mr. Hurley, who came to Palm Beach after attending to final details of Mr. Flagler's mansion in New York and the summer place in Mamaroneck.

Louise was to graduate from her kitchen job and be put in charge of the interior marble at Whitehall, which she learned later included almost every other piece of the interior—from benches to staircases. At least she would not be reporting to Mrs. Wooten.

When Jonas joined the maintenance crew of the house, he came to tell Louise the news in the hotel kitchen.

"That should make you happy. I'll be earning more money than I ever have. Maybe enough to make you change your mind about being my wife," he said. "Marry me, Louise."

Oh, Jonas, if only you knew how confused I am, she thought. I don't know where to go, and I can't marry you because I don't know what else to do.

"I don't think I can give you a palace like this," he said one afternoon as they stood before the white mansion with its over-powering pillars and huge, arched bronze and iron gate-door. "We won't live in the hut if that's what you're worried about," he said. "I can build you a fine house."

Louise shook her head from side to side. "That isn't it," she said. "I have to think."

When Jonas left her, his head lowered, Louise stood watching him disappear against a blazing gold sun.

She could not fully explain what was holding her back from Jonas' proposal. What did she want out of life anyway? To be a maid in the new mansion or someone else's house—all her life?

Carrie's words came echoing back. Carrie had made the break. Louise could create a life, a good life, with Jonas. But she never wanted to regret marrying him. She did not want to hurt Jonas now…or in the future.

When Wendell Spinner swept into Palm Beach the next day just as Mr. Flagler's house, Whitehall, was about to be stocked by trainloads of furnishings from New York, Louise was more addled than ever. He was a strange man…or boy. She could not decide which. She would have to be immune to him, ignore him completely.

"You wonder where I've been, don't you? Something came up, something I had to do. I am back for you. Pack. Go pack your bags," Wendell said, bursting into the kitchen early in the morning.

Louise began to laugh as he talked to her.

"All right," she said. "I will." She was suddenly oblivious to her surroundings, her job, the staff.

She reappeared with her valise, empty except for her mother's cross. There was no need to bring any clothes or anything else since this trip was a lark.

Wendell was waiting for her, sitting in a kitchen chair.

"Let's go," he said, taking her arm.

"Where? Where are we going?"

"I don't know, but we'll take the train, Mr. Flagler's train… north…in that direction at least."

"I'll have to tell Mr. Hurley I'm leaving. What shall I tell him?"

"Tell him you're getting married. Never mind, I'll ring him," he said, reaching for a phone and asking for a connection to Mr. Hurley's room in the hotel.

"That's right, Mr. Hurley, she is getting married to me, yes, well, thank you. I'm sure she will write you and tell you where we are."

Crazy, Wendell was crazy. For all his money, he was out of his head. She might as well go along with his joke. Of course, she would have a hard time explaining all this to Mr. Hurley, but he was an understanding man. She hoped he could stretch his imagination to digest this story.

When they arrived at the train headed for the mainland, Wendell smiled at her. "I told you I would have you, didn't I?"

It was her day off from the hotel, so she could go along for the ride on the train. She hoped he had tickets. "Where are we getting off?"

"I haven't thought about that yet. Louise," he said, pulling a small box from his pocket. "Put this on. I want us to have some kind of engagement."

Opening the box and finding a large, round diamond set in gold, Louise stared at Wendell. She was not sure he was kidding now.

"This is for me?"

"It was my grandmother's and it may not fit. But, yes, my darling, it is yours." Wendell slipped it on her finger. "It does fit, well, it's a bit loose, but you don't mind, do you? For now? We will have it sized later."

Louise was too stunned to talk. She still had time to turn back, to return the ring, and tell Wendell she would not be the object of his bizarre fun any longer.

"It's time to board," he said, moving Louise toward the steps of the train car. He reached for her hand and squeezed it.

"We're on our way...to some place to be married," he whispered. "You won't be sorry, Louise. Ever."

The Richest Woman in the World

World

A Trilogy
Book Two

by

M.G. Lambert

Bonus Chapter

As a special "thank you" gift with your purchase of this first book introducing you to Louise Lambert, we have included the first chapter of *The Richest Woman in the World - Book Two*.

Chapter 1

Palm Beach, Florida, February 10, 1902

Marriage.

It was the best idea for a girl who had no other plans in sight, wasn't it?

It seemed the worst step Louise Lambert could take—with Wendell Spinner, whom she hardly knew.

Yes, he was the son of wealth and privilege, and he was decisive and rather commanding. But what else did she know about this young man who was sitting beside her on a train whose destination Louise did not know either. Quickly, he rose and darted up the aisle ahead of them.

Wendell's brisk departure without a word to her jolted her into realizing she herself was racing into a whole other life—in many ways as frightening as the nightmare she had survived when her mother was beaten to death in the factory where she labored to support Louise and herself.

Painful memories flashed before Louise—she had been left in the streets of Lower Manhattan then, alone and destitute, with nowhere to go except a brothel where her mother had conceived her, and where Cecilia, her mother's only friend, had sought refuge for the girl until she was able to move her to a safe haven.

There were no choices then, but now...

She had not been forced to take this train from Palm Beach to some unknown place. With abandon, she had let Wendell Spinner take her hand, place a ring on her finger, and promise a wedding.

Louise had willingly walked—no run—into this wild and mysterious fantasy. Nothing around her or about the time seemed real. What force had she allowed in herself to cause her to leave her job at the Flagler mansion which had just been built for Henry Flagler's young third wife.

As a former kitchen girl in Flagler's home in New York and later at his Royal Poinciana Hotel in Palm Beach, she had been selected to manage the care of the marble of the massive structure of 75 rooms. There were tons of the smooth, shiny stone in Whitehall—from its gigantic pillars to its expansive winding interior staircases.

It would be an overwhelming job to polish and supervise the maintenance of these glistening works of art, and Louise was in awe that she would be responsible for this part of the imposing building, which was also to be her home as the servants lived at the back of Whitehall on two floors hidden in the maze of rooms.

Wasn't she fortunate to be invited to live and serve in what newspapers were calling a "palace" and "more magnificent than any private dwelling in the world"?

She was fixated on the dazzling castle behind her, the Poinciana Hotel, and the people she had come to know in Palm Beach, if only through her daily work routine. Collectively, they had filled her with a sense of belonging that was fading away.

As they headed north, Louise caught a glimpse of the station, people moving about on the platform, and then a wide open space that filled quickly with other cars. She was leaving the island, her work, her duties, her clothes, the accounting of her stock in Standard Oil—almost everything that formed her life.

Above all she was missing Jonas…and she always would.

Where had Wendell gone and why had he left her here, alone? As the train began to gain momentum, Louise's mind swirled with the people who had crowded her short life.

Cecilia—where was she? Margaret Dugal—was this monster still alive and trapping innocent girls into her den of hell? Mrs. O'Donnell, her guardian angel—she knew. Carrie—had she become a star? The policeman who took her to the Flagler mansion in New York—how would she ever find him? Mr. Hurley—would he save her position back at the Flaglers' new home? Mrs. Glenn—would she understand why Louise had fled so strangely? Ida Tarbell—was she truly writing about Standard Oil and Rockefeller and Flagler, and would her stories hurt them as Mrs. Wooten had warned?

Jonas—would he forget her, forgive her?

Yes, Mrs. Wooten and Alex, too, brooding in the shadows; she hoped they stayed there—would they dance with glee that Louise had disappeared? Wendell's parents and sister—would they punish Wendell for this madness and disown him? Mr. Flagler—how would he react when he learned that his maid had run off with one of his friend's children?

Louise counted among all of these how many of them had helped her and how many had tried to destroy her. She would make a list of the good souls she had been fortunate to meet along her way, and she would one day find them and thank each one of them in a real way—for her life.

To an onlooker, Louise appeared to have just about everything—she was beautiful, she was young, she wore a stunning diamond ring, she had a fiancé, and together they seemed to be embarking on an exciting life.

She wished Wendell were here. Why had he wandered away? She had to know where they were headed. They had no tickets, and if the conductor approached her, especially if Wendell had not returned, she could not explain her presence on the train.

Wendell was suddenly standing before her, waving their tickets and talking so fast she could not fully understand him. "I had to book us into our hotel in St. Augustine and get these," she heard him say.

"St. Augustine?"

"Yes, we will be married there as soon as we arrive. I have reserved the bridal suite at the Ponce de Leon, made dinner reservations, and planned our honeymoon. Everything. You'll see..."

"Wendell, this is happening so fast, I, I am not ready..."

"Leave it all to me, Louise," Wendell said without looking at the girl. He pulled out a small, flat, silver container, unscrewed the top, and held the bottle to his lips and drank.

"Ah, this will solve it all," he said under his breath. "Nothing like a sip now and then." He smiled and reached for Louise's hand, which she pulled away.

It was whisky that she smelled, and as he took another drink and another, he began to smile without stopping that either.

"Dinner, no, lunch I guess, we will have in a few minutes in the dining car and then in a few hours we hit Jacksonville and will be taken by carriage to the hotel, which Mr. Flagler also built. It is not so grand as the Poinciana, but it was decorated by Tiffany himself, Louis Comfort, whose stained glass windows alone make the hotel world famous. The bridal suite is glorious I am told…"

Wendell rattled on and on and then he fell asleep, the silver flask resting on his lap and then falling to the floor. Louise picked it up, opened it, and smelled the liquor. It was alarmingly familiar, and it sickened her. It contained more of the whisky. She clutched it, put it in her small bag, and brushed past Wendell, who did not move as she made her exit.

In the restroom at the end of their car, she shook the small bottle and poured the remainder of the whisky down the sink. She could not tolerate his drinking.

When she arrived back at their seats, Wendell was still asleep, his mouth open, the stench of his liquor breath making her queasy. She left the empty bottle in his lap, sat down, breathed a sigh of relief, and studied Wendell's profile. He was so young and slight, hardly a man. She studied his soft hands—he had never worked as had the men she had known or met. He had been served and pampered and given everything he had ever wanted.

Wendell awoke, squinted his eyes against the rays of the sun casting yellow streaks across the seats from the west, and reached for his whisky. Shaking the container, he realized it was empty.

"My god, I drank all of it. Well, it's time to eat. Let's go to lunch. I'm famished. You must be, too, my bride."

The dining car's tables were set with crisp white linens and small vases of red roses. Louise could not quite grasp that she was here and would be served by the waiters who moved about the car taking orders.

"Rare roast beef au jus, au gratin potatoes, fresh green peas, and your best aged Cabernet Sauvignon, your largest bottle, good sir," Wendell told the server. "This is a celebration of our wedding."

"Sir," said the waiter, "we serve complimentary champagne for newlyweds, a gift from Mr. Henry Flagler. Do you want the wine with dinner or..."

"Yes, the wine with dinner and the champagne later. And thank Mr. Flagler for us. Or I will. He is a family friend."

"Indeed, that is fine," the waiter said, nodding.

"You do like roast beef, Louise, and everything I ordered, I hope. You will learn that I like to select foods and wines. My father usually decides everything for us. But not any more. Not any more," Wendell's voice trailed off as if he were making a major statement to his father, not to Louise.

Wendell approached his food not with a ravenous energy but with the measured movements of someone who had been carefully instructed in proper table manners.

She copied the way he used his silver, slicing his roast beef in only bite-sized pieces, one at a time; using his butter knife and placing it back at an angle on his bread plate. Although Louise had eaten fine food in the Flagler staff kitchens, she had never sat at a formal table and did not feel comfortable about cutting meat or fish, how to hold her flatware, how to select the right fork or spoon or knife for each course. And so Wendell had to be her teacher, even if he was unaware of the girl's ignorance of such things.

Louise only sipped the wine from her big goblet and barely tasted the sparkling champagne after dinner. The bubbles tickled her nose, and the taste of the festive drink slightly lifted her thoughts above her latest worry, Wendell's drinking. He continued with after-dinner bright amber cognac, swishing it around from side to side in its gleaming, clear glass brandy snifter. He finally drank it all, and asked the waiter to fill his flask with more whisky. "My nightcap," he quipped and handed the Negro waiter some folded bills.

Wendell placed the flask in his suit pocket and slept while Louise tried to reason out what she should do next. She had a few dollars in her bag, and if she could retrieve her valise, she could leave the train at the next stop and get back to Palm Beach.

She could not go on to Jacksonville with no clothes, no credentials to marry—even if she tried to go through with Wendell's plans. She felt of the ring on her left hand. She could use the ring if she absolutely had to. Sell it, pawn it, but where and how? She might be accused of stealing such a big diamond.

"Next stop is Jacksonville," called the conductor as he strode up and down the aisle of the train car. Wendell did not awaken or even move. Louise motioned to the conductor and asked if she could have her valise. She had given it to a porter when she boarded back in Palm Beach and saw that it was ticketed but had no proof, she explained.

"Come with me," the conductor said and motioned to her to follow him to the front of the car where some luggage was stored. Luckily, her small brown case was on top of the stacks of suitcases. She took it back to a seat in front of Wendell and waited.

As the train slowed and rolled into the station, Louise rose, not looking back at Wendell, and walked quickly to the front of the car and waited in a front seat. When the train had come to a complete stop, she almost bolted to the door, which was opened by a conductor, who paused and asked if her groom was coming along.

Louise smiled without answering.

"Yes, he is coming along," Wendell blurted out just behind Louise. "This bride is going nowhere without her groom."

Shocked at Wendell's quick appearance behind her, Louise held her valise tightly in front of her.

"Yes, sir, yes, ma'am," said a porter who moved the luggage down the steps of the car and onto the platform where he hailed one of the carriage drivers meeting arriving passengers.

"We have a carriage waiting, my good man," Wendell told the attendant, saw a driver with a sign with his name, and waved to the man to fetch his case and Louise's.

As they entered the carriage, Wendell took Louise's hand. "You tried to run away from me, didn't you, my bride? You must not do that again. Not ever. You are about to be my wife. What kind of honeymoon is this?" His face was stern and his eyes, alarming.

"I, I am confused, Wendell. I have no way of getting married. No identification..."

"Don't worry about that. I have a justice of the peace who knows that your birth certificate was burned last year in that horrible fire in Jacksonville. In May of last year it destroyed 1,700 buildings, including some of ours, and your records are all gone. You are 18 now and your birthday was on February 1st. I have covered everything. You need some whisky."

Louise was silent on the question of her birth. She had never had a birth certificate so Wendell was establishing why, and she counted his story of deception to her advantage.

Wendell reached for his flask, laughed, and sat back in the carriage for the ride to St. Augustine.

A cool afternoon breeze greeted them as they rode in the open carriage out of Jacksonville and to the town that claimed to be America's oldest city, founded in 1565 by the Spanish. When Flagler saw St. Augustine, he decided to make it the American

Riviera and built the Ponce de Leon Hotel there, opening it in early 1888. The luxury retreat was a smashing success and drew Northern visitors down right away to escape the bitter cold of the East.

As they approached the imposing hotel, Louise was reminded of the Poinciana, not because of its likeness to this Flagler creation, but because of its dominance over the landscape. These buildings were reddish in the fading gold sunlight, their spires rising above patches of fan-shaped palmettos and tall oak trees draped with hanging gray moss.

"Spanish Mission style," Wendell said "Wait till you see the interiors. Thomas Edison, Henry's friend, brought electricity to this hotel. Has 540 rooms, small by Poinciana standards."

Louise's mind wandered to the rooms of the Poinciana Hotel, and she tried to guess how many maids and cooks and waiters it took to serve the guests here, at the Ponce de Leon. But what did all this matter now? She would not be working here—or would she? She might have to earn enough money to escape Wendell.

"You know I have no clothes for a wedding, Wendell."

"I have solved that. I know the main shopkeeper here, and she has chosen your dress and trousseau. She is waiting for us now. While you change, I will call the justice who will marry us in a special events room off the rotunda—wait till you see it—and then we will feast in the great dining hall before taking our bridal suite on an upper floor. It will be heaven."

Or hell, Louise thought. How and when can I leave him? I cannot go through with this farce. It is a play, a drama. She wished Carrie were here to see it as Louise played the damsel in distress. The audience would sit on the edges of their seats for this bizarre tragicomedy.

Before she knew it, Louise was entering the hotel and staring up at the overpowering, light wood rotunda which encased another smaller, identical rotunda.

Natural light surrounded the dome above, flooding the entrance with the last sunrays of the day. Cherubs, Greek figures, lion heads, and artwork she could not place decorated every wall, every space.

In a small shop off the lobby, Louise found herself meeting a small, dark-haired woman who held before her a white lace gown covered with seed pearls from bodice to hem.

"This, my dear one, is your wedding gown. And it looks as though it will be a perfect fit. Let me see." Miss Grace, as she called herself, measured Louise's waist and arms. "Yes, Mr. Wendell was quite right about you. It is perfect. I will assist you in dressing, and Mr. Wendell has ordered other attire. Some daywear and shoes and undergarments. But, first, the wedding tonight. And I am invited. An honor."

Louise's impulse was to run now as fast as she could, but something held her back. This was not the right time. Later, later, she told herself, when Wendell least expected it.

Looking at herself in the large wall mirror of the Grace Shop, Louise had to admit the dress was breathtaking, and she was lovely, yes, lovely wearing it. A picture—like some of those magazine covers Carrie had made her study. Was this all just an illusion, some imaginary tale?

Standing before the justice of the peace, a tall, thin man with sparse gray hair, Louise began to shake. Wendell steadied her hands, and together they said their vows, repeating the words of the justice.

"I do," Louise heard herself saying as if she were another person.

Wendell slipped a wedding band on her finger. It matched the gold of the big diamond engagement ring.

Then he kissed the bride on cue.

They were married.

It was done. Louise felt a quivering sensation race through her body as the couple turned and greeted Miss Grace and a few men who Wendell later explained were staff of the hotel.

Miss Grace led Louise back to her shop where Louise changed into a royal blue satin gown with matching shoes and evening bag.

"Now, madame, you are ready for your wedding dinner. Your evening bridal attire will be waiting for you in your suite. My, what a treasure you have in your hands. You are so lucky, Miss Louise, to marry a member of the Spinner family. They have been guests here for years. Friends of Mr. Flagler."

"Yes, yes, I know," Louise managed to answer. If only this woman knew the facts about her, about Wendell. She would be astounded.

Without exception, the dining room guests stared and smiled at the couple as they made their way to the center of the multi-columned dining complex with its vaulted, highly decorated ceilings and long tables.

The young Spinners created a painting of Gilded Age splendor. Handsome, exquisitely dressed, young, rich, proper.

What contradictory images to the truth, Louise thought.

I have to run away tonight and find my way back to my job as a servant and to the only security I have known since my life with my mother in that small, dingy flat with no electric lights—our home.

Their dinner was a spectacular array from croquettes of shrimp to broiled chad to simple grilled lamb chops with miniature green peas and on to the crowning glory of the meal, a puffy vanilla soufflé. All followed by champagne.

Wendell had ordered wine with every course and ended the evening celebration with a brandy. He also asked the waiter to fill his flask with whisky for his "nightcap."

He looked at Louise, pausing. "You are magnificent in that dress. The deep blue matches your eyes perfectly. But then you are gorgeous in anything. Or without anything," he smiled.

Louise found his compliments grating.

After dinner, their exclusive valet led them to their suite, which Wendell had filled with red and pink roses which perfumed the rooms.

On the high four-poster bed lay an assortment of white satin and silk nightgowns, slippers, and what seemed more lingerie than a shop would stock.

A silver bucket stood on a large, round table in the center of the suite, and in minutes a room service waiter delivered a magnum of French champagne and ice.

Wendell waved the server away with bills and said they would serve themselves and pop the cork later.

Lifting his empty champagne glass in jest, Wendell toasted his bride. "Louise, I love you, I love you." His words were slurred, and he could hardly walk as he made his way toward her, swung an arm around her waist, and dropped his glass.

"We will have the champagne later. For breakfast. Right now, I am going to be sick," he said, finding his way to the bathroom.

Louise was relieved when he left her.

She dressed in one of the fancy gowns and propped herself up on a stack of pillows covered in white cotton-and-lace cases.

Now it was time to plan her escape.

Wendell's illness could not have been more advantageous for her.

When Wendell came to Louise, he fell at the foot of the bed. "I need to sleep now," he said. He appeared to have passed out. His body lay sprawled out across the far end of the high mattress.

Louise buried her head in the pillows and cried herself to sleep. She was too tired to run and too confused to think.

Wendell did not stir during the night. Her prayers were answered but not complete—she now asked to be forgiven for making such an unwise decision to follow Wendell into what she knew was a doomed alliance.

Within seconds of awakening in the morning, Louise was startled by a loud banging on the heavy double doors of the suite.

"Wendell, I know you're in there. Open this door. Immediately. Or I will break it down," came the thundering sound of a man's voice. "It's your father."

www.ingramcontent.com/pod-product-compliance
Lightning Source LLC
Chambersburg PA
CBHW071915220626
47052CB00002B/361